Barber-osophy

Barber-osophy—

Hair We Go Again

Terry L. Sumerlin

Publishing
S E Publishing • San Antonio, Texas

Barber-osophy—
Hair We Go Again

By Terry L. Sumerlin

Cover art: Holly Hein
Cover Graphics: Michael Qualben

Copyright © 2004 Terry L. Sumerlin
First Printing: 2004
Printed in the United States of America

Published by
S E Publishing
6338 N. New Braunfels, PMB 180
San Antonio, Texas 78209

Library of Congress Cataloging-in-Publication Data in Process

ISBN: 09659662-1-6   USA $12.95

Dedication

To Lola Sanders, my beloved grandmother, who taught me to love good books, and to her daughter—my mother Darlene, who with my father, Eddie, always believed in me.

A SPECIAL THANK YOU to my dear friend and consultant, Lois Qualben, whose invaluable work and guidance made this book possible.

TABLE OF CONTENTS

The Barber-osopher's Creed for Better Living 9
Prologue 11

SHEER SUCCESS IN BUILDING RELATIONSHIPS

The Lady and the Llama 15
Stop Banging That Drum 17
Like Riding in the Back of a Pickup 19
The Part That No One Notices 21
Two Cases of Blown Cover 23
When a New Acquaintance Becomes a Pest 25
The Bashful Buzzard Complex 27
Rewards of an Open Heart 29
Having Something to Say Versus Having to Say 31

GROOMING THE HEART FOR SUCCESS

A Mountain of Success 37
A Rags to Riches Story 39
Flat Tires, Pyramids and Greatness 41
Pleasant Memories of "Cousin Ernie" 43
Quality, Not Quantity, Is What Counts in Life 45
The Tale of Three Bulls 47
When Exceptions Rule 49

THE CUTTING EDGE IN SALES AND SERVICE

No Vacancy 53
Coffee and a Tip 55
A Buzz in the Parking Lot 57
Clear-Headed Business Philosophy 59
Customer Meltdown 61
Who's Next? 63
The Unappreciated Customer 65
Common Sense Business Debts 67
Three Requirements for Attracting & Keeping People .. 69

GROWTH STIMULATORS

The Upside-Down Tree 75

"It's a Churchill Thing" 77
Livin' on "Someday I'll" 79
When the Zeroes Don't Add Up 81
Painful Lessons 83
Advice Can Be Fishy 85
Teacher, Teacher, I Declare 87
I Confess—I Slipped in Under the Fence 89
River Ramblings 91
An All-too-Common Addiction 93
Vote Against Indifference 96
Getting Personal About Commitment 99

WHEN THINGS GET HAIRY

The Sunrise of a New Day 103
One at a Time 105
The Door to Happiness 107
A Terminal Connection 109
Those Boils on the Neck 111
J.B.'s Barber Shop and Sauna 113
Coasting to Crisis Management 115
Doggin' It 117

TOOLS FOR A HAPPY HOME

A Practical Guide to a Better Marriage 121
"Everything I Need to Know About Raising Kids..." .. 124
A Generation of Hotdogs 126
You've Gotta Love It 128
A Few Thoughts From the Hill 130
Out of the Mouths of Babes 132
If Grandpa Did It 134
If It's Good—Savor It 136
A Little Seasoning 138

CUTTING UP

The Assault of Humor 143
Humor Can Be a Funny Thing 146
Caution—Amateur at Work! 148
Enough is Enough 151
Jump Start a Smile 152
When We are Blind-sided by Miscommunication 154
Useless (but fun) Information 156

THE BARBEROSOPHER'S CREED FOR BETTER LIVING

TODAY *I will not whine or complain. Unlike one who says he feels bad even on days when he feels good, for fear he'll feel worse tomorrow; I'll expose others to a positive attitude worth catching.*

TODAY *I will not talk about my health, except in a general, positive way. I'll spare others an organ recital.*

TODAY *I will talk in terms of the other person's interest, and, when possible, seek to eliminate "I" from my conversation.*

TODAY *I will encourage all who need encouragement. I will determine who needs encouragement merely by checking to see who is breathing.*

TODAY *I will dress for the occasion and out of respect for others, rather than simply for selfish reasons and comfort. I will keep in mind that if I dress like I just got out of bed, I will tend to feel and act like it.*

TODAY *I will go the second mile, knowing that those who do more than they are paid to do will someday (by someone) be paid more for what they do.*

TODAY *I will live with enthusiasm, realizing that as I can make myself happy by singing I can also be enthusiastic by acting that way. I will pick my head up, look others in the eye, give them a firm handshake, call them by name and* **smile.**

TODAY *I will speak my opinion sparingly and give advice only when asked, keeping in mind the proverb that says, "A fool speaks all his mind."*

TODAY *I will build relationships instead of walls. Life is too precious for pettiness.*

TODAY *I will not gossip. Words have wings, and there is no telling where they will land.*

TODAY *if I must talk to someone about my personal problems, I will find a leader rather than someone who takes their lead from me. That way I will not shake a follower's confidence in me.*

TODAY *I will learn something new, even if it means giving up an idea I thought was valid. I will avoid the type of mind that's like concrete—all mixed up and permanently set.*

TODAY *I will remember the words of Mark Twain: "Against the assault of laughter nothing can stand."*

TODAY *I will live as "a human becoming," determined to become more than I was yesterday.*

Prologue

On July 25th, 1996 Sherry and I celebrated our twenty-seventh wedding anniversary. That day, J.B.'s Barber Shop celebrated its fortieth anniversary.

The shop is located in the San Antonio suburb of Alamo Heights and has served four generations of area residents. It's a south-central Texas institution.

To enter J.B.'s Barber Shop is to return to our past. It's a world of buzzes, flattops, regular haircuts and bubble gum. Of sixty-year-old barber chairs, animals heads, a 1951 Admiral television set, seven-foot steer horns and memorabilia of all sorts. Regular customers are called by name and have an opportunity to chat with friends and business associates. Newcomers can hardly believe all this still exists.

My Uncle J.B., my dad's younger brother, sold the shop to me March 4, 1993, and is now semi-retired, working three days a week. I also work in the barber-shop, when not engaged in writing or on the road sharing common-sense business and life lessons as The Barber-osopher.

Shear Success in

Building

Relationships

BARBER-OSOPHY: "When dealing with others, there's no substitute for the three "C's"— common sense, courtesy and consideration."

THE LADY AND THE LLAMA

In *Barber-osophy — Shear Success for Your Cutting Edge*, I tell the story of the day a customer brought a llama into J.B.'s Barber Shop. Though people find the story hard to believe, it really happened. What follows also really happened.

While I was doing a book signing in Corpus Christi, Texas in walked a rather attractive lady wearing a white jacket and a pager. I was flattered when she immediately took an interest in my book, and asked if I would inscribe it to her and autograph it.

After I handed the book back to the lady, we chatted for a minute. Then she began to browse and to make her selections. Occasionally she would walk by my table, and we would chat some more.

At one point when she walked near me, I noticed that she had about a dozen books. I commented that she must really like to read. She simply responded that they were not all for her.

The lady must have spent an hour in the store looking at and collecting books. All the while, I was feeling pretty good over the idea that this attractive, well-educated professional found my book suited to her very discriminating taste.

Wrong! As my adoring public left the store, the manager was right behind her. My book, along with the others, was brought back into the store—to be *sold*.

I've often wondered how much they got for the book inscribed to my fan. Regardless, "the lady *and* the llama" both teach us the same valuable lesson:

BARBER-OSOPHY: Expect people to do the unexpected.

Stop Banging That Drum

I read that, nowadays, educated people don't come right out and ask others what they do for a living. First of all, to do so shows that the inquirer is likely unaware that some folks are independently wealthy and choose not to do anything. Secondly, it could be embarrassing for one who is unemployed and has to answer such a question. The author suggested it's better to ask, "How do you spend most of your time?" Such an open-ended question leaves people free to answer any way they choose. And, it also stimulates conversation.

After reading this suggestion, I decided to give it a try with a longtime customer. He had recently retired from a job that regularly took him to Baltimore and to Washington, D.C. I had never heard him speak of hobbies and was curious as to how he would spend his time since he would no longer have to travel. His answer surprised and pleased me. "I'm going to college," he said.

Knowing he was already very well educated, I couldn't imagine what he might be studying. Come to find out, he's a percussionist majoring in music at the University of Texas at San Antonio. Suddenly, we had something most interesting to talk about. I played drums in high school and, at one time, had plans to become a band director. The customer and I are now bound by paradiddles (one of the 26 drum rudiments). The conversational technique really worked.

Yet, as a spin-off of my limited musical training, I've discovered another technique that works well in human relations. It involves something that was drilled into my head by my first band director at Terrell Wells Middle School in San Antonio. Because she, too, had been a drummer, she was an excellent teacher when it came to the snare drum.

Since most young drummers want to *bang* on the drum, one of the things she taught us was, "Drums are to be *felt*, not heard." In other words, they are not to be intrusive, annoying or obvious. As I listen to music, I'm often reminded of her instructions. Her words also come to mind as they relate to the human relations technique I mentioned.

It was much more fun to learn something unexpected from the customer; instead of having him boldly announce everything he's doing, as if he were banging on a drum. Yet, it's so easy for you and me, by constantly "banging on our drum," to deprive another of the joy of discovering something new about us. While we are busy beating our drum, it never occurs to us to make the other person feel important by simply asking, "How do you spend most of your time?"

BARBER-OSOPHY: Learning about others is often more rewarding than informing others about self.

Like Riding in the Back of a Pickup

One of the things I was taught very early in life was to be careful what I asked people. In fact, there are some things I was taught not to ask at all.

For instance, you don't ask adults, and in particular ladies, their age. The same is true of inquiring where someone bought something and how much he paid for it.

Such questions are usually not a sign of good manners or of proper upbringing. Even today I find myself guarding my questions, both in and out of the barbershop. But I sometimes slip.

Apparently others were not brought up the same way, however. Most of us hear evidence of this all the time.

While Sherry, Jon and I were eating in a restaurant one day after work, a stranger walked over to us. With absolutely no hesitation at all, he said to me, "I hope you don't think I'm being too forward, but do you put something on your head to make it shine or does it just shine naturally?"

Seldom am I at a loss for words, but on this occasion I was. I was so shocked by such gall, I simply muttered something about not putting anything on my head.

Then I turned to my wife and son, who were as flabber-gasted as I was, and muttered that I couldn't believe what had just happened.

I have often thought how similar that man's statement was to: "I hope you don't think I'm too violent, but may I hit you in the face?" But, then, how would you frame the fellow's question any better than *he* did? I guess the stranger did the best he could with what he had to work with.

To ask some questions is about like riding in the back end of a pickup. It's hard to show a great deal of class while doing so.

BARBER-OSOPHY: Questions have a way of revealing class or a lack of it.

The Part That No One Notices

I once had a customer in an assisted living facility. He had been a longtime customer. So, when he was unable to come in for his haircut, I went to his facility. It was a small thing to do for such a loyal customer, but he seemed to really appreciate it.

One day while I was cutting his hair, he said: "Terry, I think I'm going to quit trying to part my hair and just comb it straight back. I get in the bathroom in front of the mirror and just can't see what I'm doing."

I told him I thought it would look fine that way and then added, "I think that even without the part, they'll still let you eat in the dining room." He kind of chuckled and then responded, "I don't think anyone in there will know whether I *have* a part or not."

Though his comment apparently referred to the age of the residents and was an exaggeration, it contained some common sense. I suspect there are lots of folks even outside that facility who wouldn't notice whether he had a part or not.

Along this line, it seems many people worry a great deal about things no one else notices or would care about even if they did notice. After all, they're worried about what they think we're noticing about *them*.

This, by the way, is the root of self-consciousness. It's when a person's thoughts are constantly turned inward, and when we think everyone is looking at us, scrutinizing everything about us, or judging us.

What is the cure? While I'm not a psychologist, and certainly not perfect, I think that at least a partial cure might come in the form of an experiment. See if you can remember what any two of your co-workers wore yesterday. If you can't, consider two possibilities. (1) They probably weren't noticing a great deal about you either. (2) They might notice more about you if you made it a point to pay more attention to them. In the process, any self-consciousness you might have will start to disappear.

BARBER-OSOPHY: Those who are concerned about being noticed rarely attract as much attention as those who make it a point to take note of others.

Two Cases of Blown Cover

"I'm very important. I'm an astronaut, and I went up on the last mission." That's what someone might have been tempted to say had he (she) been the one seated next to me at a banquet. However, the person next to me showed much more class.

As we chatted, I asked how he spends his time. He simply responded that he worked for NASA. Then while we were visiting about Clear Lake, Texas, where NASA is located, a lady walked up and asked me if I knew I was seated next to an astronaut.

The astronaut seemed very embarrassed and gently told the lady that we were not there to talk about him. As he and I continued visiting, however, he did tell me he went up on the previous mission.

Recently I thought of this while chatting with a customer. When I called his name, it was a tip-off to another customer as to the identity of the man I was working on. So, they began to get reacquainted. As it turned out, my customer is also a barber with an outstanding clientele that he has served for over thirty years. Though he had been coming into J.B.'s for several years, he never told me he is a barber. And, he had never been particular about his haircut. I commented to him that if I had known he was a barber (and one who has been at it much longer than I), I would have really felt the pressure. His reply was very impressive: "That's why I didn't tell you." It made me a little sorry that the other customer had unwittingly blown the barber's cover.

Both the barber and the astronaut showed an unselfishness that is refreshing. Both of them were other-person minded and sought to put me at ease.

Someone has observed that the person who is all wrapped up in himself makes a mighty small package. Neither of these men would fit that description. But, what about the rest of us?

BARBER-OSOPHY: We are most impressive when we're not trying to be.

WHEN A NEW ACQUAINTANCE BECOMES A PEST

How I wish I had perfect human relations both inside and outside of the barbershop. Then I would never feel like a jerk over how I treated someone, as I did over an incident that happened one morning on the way to the shop.

I had been stopping at a certain restaurant every Saturday morning, and a fellow I had seen there apparently decided we needed to start bonding. He ate there with a group every Saturday morning, and we had merely said "hello" on several occasions.

One day he made it a point to introduce himself. Then the following week, he invited himself to my table, sat for 45 minutes and proceeded to ask personal questions while waiting for his group to arrive. He did this despite the fact I was sitting there with a book in hand, doing what he had repeatedly seen me do—read. But, this time I tried to be courteous.

A few Saturdays later, he got out of his car in the eatery's parking lot at the same time I exited my car. He followed me to the door. As we were entering, he asked about the book I was carrying. He then walked to my table, as if invited, and was about to join me again.

What followed is what made me feel like a bum. In frustration, I simply told him he was welcome to sit where he chose, but that I was intent on reading my book. He said, "Good day" and made his way to another table.

Yet, in spite of the fact I felt like a jerk, is privacy too much to ask?

In retrospect, it is easy to see that the fellow is likely a good person who thought he was just being friendly. Or, maybe he had some sort of agenda he was leading up to. Regardless, it seemed he had some training in how to meet and talk to people.

It makes me wonder, though, if in connection with all that has been spoken and written concerning human relations, assertiveness and self-image, maybe we have omitted things like common sense, courtesy and consideration.

BARBER-OSOPHY: When dealing with others, there is no substitute for the three "C's"—common sense, courtesy and consideration.

The Bashful Buzzard Complex

The announcer on the shop's radio was talking to a man on the phone.

"So today's your thirty-first wedding anniversary?"

"Yes, it is."

"Wow! That's great. How'd you manage to stay married so long?"

After a bit of delay, all the fellow could say was, "We just started out."

We just started out??? Nothing about commitment, sacrifice or work? That's about like saying, "One day this company hired me. Then I just started showing up for work every day. Next thing I knew, they were giving me a gold watch for having shown up for fifty years."

Maybe the caller was just caught off guard or was stumped. On the other hand, maybe he didn't know how to receive a compliment. If that were the case, he's not alone.

Many times in watching folks receive compliments, I'm reminded of a cartoon that I saw on TV when I was growing up. It showed a "mama" buzzard trying to teach her young to fly. She took them to a high cliff and coaxed each one into flapping his wings and taking to the air. Each one, that is, except the last one. He was not to be persuaded. Each time he got to the edge, he would tuck his head under his wing and, in a bashful sort of way, say, "Nope. Nope. I can't do it. I can't do it."

When complimented, we often do somewhat the same thing. Someone says, "Bob, you did a great job on that report."

Bob then ducks his head and says, "Nope. Nope. Not me. It was nothing."

"Susan, your presentation at the manager's meeting was fantastic."

"Nope. Nope. I was scared to death. Couldn't you tell?"

On and on we could go with such illustrations. Yet, they all have one thing in common. They are often manifestations of a low self-image.

Confident individuals, on the other hand, generally respond to compliments with eye contact, a smile and a simple "Thank you very much."

Yet, there is something else that confident people often do. They often *give* compliments. With the same eye contact and smile, they praise the person for something very specific. One of the most effective ways to do this is to begin with "you."

"You look very nice today in that color." That is far better than, "Nice suit." The latter is often perceived more as flattery than as a compliment.

When a remark is perceived as a compliment, though it cost nothing, it becomes priceless. It also becomes a gift that the recipient will open repeatedly.

BARBER-OSOPHY: People with class have learned how to give and to receive the gift of a compliment.

Rewards of an Open Heart

The most rewarding thing about writing is knowing that someone takes the time to read what you've written. So, I deeply appreciate you, the reader.

I also appreciate a comment that a customer made concerning *Barber-osophy — Shear Success for Your Cutting Edge*.

"It must have been very difficult to open up like that." I found the comment very interesting.

I don't think he meant that the book is some sort of exposé. He seemed to simply be saying that he thought I was honest about strengths, weaknesses, likes and dislikes. I guess he found this refreshing.

Benjamin Franklin said: "If you would not be forgotten, either write things worth reading, or do things worth writing." However, Barber-osophy has taught me that something doesn't have to be earthshaking to be worth reading. Apparently it just has to come from the heart.

Generally, people are uncomfortable when forced to listen to intimate details of others' lives. Yet, conversely, we are often put off by those who are ultraprivate. They seem to be intimidating. Openness, on the other hand, tends to build relationships.

Openness has benefits beyond readability and relationships—it's a great release!

The facade we often carry around can become very heavy. As a speaker, when asked about my day job, for years I would respond by saying: "I own a small business." "I'm self-employed." "I'm involved in several things." I was afraid if I revealed that I'm a barber, my vocation might not seem impressive enough. Now, as I speak, I find great satisfaction in being The Barber-osopher. And, The Barber-osopher often says from the platform that if we are what we do, then when we don't, we aren't.

BARBER-OSOPHY: Never hide who you are or what you do.

Having Something to Say
Versus Having to Say Something

Just before leaving for the local Madison-Judson high school football game, Sherry entered our office to check the e-mails. I had settled into the recliner when she called out.

"Someone sent you an e-mail wanting to know what happened to your column for next week."

At first I didn't know what she was talking about, because I thought my submissions to a San Antonio paper were current. Come to find out, I had not checked my calendar, and I was a column short.

Regardless of the cause of the problem, I needed to solve it—quickly. I had to decide what to write about.

I started to write about the two whiskey barrels on each side of the door outside the barbershop. They are both full of beautiful flowers most of the time and add to the warmth of our business. J.B. has a green thumb and for years has done a wonderful job of tending to these flowers. But, that's about all that came to mind about flowers.

I even thought I might write about the novel I'm working on. However, I decided I ought to finish reading it first.

Deer season had just opened. But I quit hunting years ago, and I hadn't heard any stories from customers.

Then I thought that maybe something about the SBC Center, the new home for the San Antonio Spurs, would interest folks. It's supposed to be very nice. I hadn't been there, though, and really hadn't done the research necessary to render an opinion about the facility.

I had nothing to write about.

Then I thought that not all is lost. It could be there is something to be said about the restraint to be exercised when one has nothing to talk about. The column started coming together.

As a reader, though, you're probably a bit frustrated as you read my mindless ramblings. I sometimes wonder if people feel that way when we talk just to break the silence. Or when conversation is more a stream of consciousness than it is an intelligible, meaningful means of communication.

Contrary to what we might think, silence can be a good thing. It doesn't necessarily mean a person is sick, angry or antisocial. It might merely suggest the person knows about certain things and doesn't know about other things. It could be that person has an opinion on some things, and on other things has no opinion at all.

Most of all, silence might suggest a need to think! Too often the correlation between thinking and speaking is merely coincidental. Generally, the person for whom this is not the case is the person who speaks when he has something to say and, as a result, is usually considered intelligent.

BARBER-OSOPHY: If we want people to listen when we speak, we must make it a habit to speak only when we have something to say.

Grooming the

Heart for

Success

BARBER-OSOPHY: "Where the heart leads,
we naturally follow."

A Mountain of Success

One morning, while working on a haircut, I was taken back to my boyhood by a song that was playing on the radio behind my chair. I was also inspired by a story Sherry told me about the song.

Sherry said (So, I know it's true!) that when the singer recorded what was in those days the "A" side of the record, the producer asked if he had something to put on the "B" side. He said he didn't. The producer persisted by asking if there was *anything* he might be working on that they could use. He said it really didn't matter what it was, since no one paid any attention to the "B" side of a record anyway.

Rather sheepishly the singer said that he was working on something, but he thought it was a rather dumb song. The producer asked him to sing a few lines. So, he sang: "They say don't go, on Wolverton Mountain…" The producer agreed that it was dumb, but said it would do.

Today, no one knows what is on the "A" side of the incredible hit of yesterday. It was completely overshadowed by "Wolverton Mountain."

Many might say that the singer, Claude King, was unbelievably lucky for such to have happened. Yet, without the unheralded work that went into the "A" side of the record, there would never have been the "other side."

BARBER-OSOPHY: Luck is often the flip side of hard work.

A Rags to Riches Story

Several weeks ago, a longtime friend and I met at the Riverwalk Marriott snack area, where we had soup and sandwiches for lunch.

Why there? Since I did the inviting, I also did the picking. And, I'm partial to that hotel.

Many years ago I worked at that Marriott. And, it represents the beginning of a long, fulfilling journey.

As a result of hearing Zig Ziglar tell the story of Johnny, the shoeologist in the St. Louis airport, I made a decision. I would own shoeshine stands all over San Antonio, and it would be the biggest and best such operation in the country.

So, Sherry and I lovingly designed an elaborate oak stand and found an excellent furniture maker to craft the lovely stand for us. It was then moved into the Marriott, where I went to work with shine rags, dressed in much the same manner as The Barber-osospher.

I had a ball and met many interesting people. However, it did not generate the income I had envisioned. In the fall of 1989, when J.B. approached me at a family reunion and asked me to go to work for him, the timing was perfect and I accepted.

But, the Riverwalk Marriott and the few people that I know who still work there have a very special place in my heart.

While at the shine stand, customers would sometimes pick up on the fact that maybe I was a bit over-qualified for the role of a shoeshine man. So, they would ask, "What are *you* doing here?" Usually, I would answer with a version of the Ziglar story.

What I should have said was: "I'm living an entrepreneurial dream until a better dream comes along." And, it has! It didn't work out as a shoeologist, but, The Barber-osopher is alive and well and enjoying riches in the form of fulfillment.

BARBER-OSOPHY: We take the dignity and the dream to the job.

FLAT TIRES, PYRAMIDS, AND GREATNESS

Many of our customers know that we're a baseball family. That's about the only sport I care much about. When asked about the Spurs, I say that, though I rarely go to games, I pull for them and want to see the nice guys finish first.

One issue of *Reader's Digest* had a great cover story about one of their nice guys—David Robinson. I've mentioned the story to a number of customers and have received a couple of stories in return. I think you will find them refreshing.

One customer told of driving to the airport. As he was going up I-37, he noticed a lady on the shoulder, beside her car. The car had a flat. As drivers passed they were honking and waving at the gentleman who was changing the tire. It was David Robinson.

The other story involves a very prominent local businessman whom David Robinson invited to his home for dinner. Like me, the guest knows nothing about basketball. So, he was naturally concerned about carrying on a conversation. The businessman did some research and tried to be at least slightly knowledgeable about the sport. He found that his homework had been largely for nothing because in all the time he was in Mr. Robinson's home, the topic of basketball never came up.

The *Reader's Digest* article to which I referred involves the same attitudes as our two stories—selflessness and service. It talks of how David Robinson has made the single largest charitable contribution of any professional athlete in history. He gave five million dollars to build the Carver Academy. He said he wants to make a difference in kids' lives.

If it were possible to diagram greatness, I believe it would be in the form of an inverted pyramid. The truly great are represented at the bottom, with those they serve on top. The larger the pyramid, the greater the number served—and the greater the servant!

BARBER-OSOPHY: We never stand taller than when we stoop to help another.

Pleasant Memories of "Cousin Ernie"

One day as a customer got out of the chair, he handed me a one hundred dollar bill. When I explained to him that I didn't have change, another customer quickly came to the rescue.

After the customer left, the obliging fellow stood at my chair and, with a great deal of embarrassment, asked, "You know what I just did? I left myself with just this hundred dollar bill to pay you with."

When I read of the passing of Ernie Schriever, I thought of this and of how we used to laugh when I would remind him of the incident.

He told me of another embarrassing occasion when he walked up to a lady who he thought was an employee of his famous San Antonio department store and told her that she was not allowed to chew gum in the store. He later discovered the lady didn't work for him —she was a customer.

Another time he picked up a customer's packages and carried them out to the car for her. She thought he was simply an employee and was flabbergasted when she discovered he was *Mr. Schriever.*

However, to those who heard his radio ads (which he wrote) and to his barber, he was "Cousin Ernie." He remains one of the most youthful and generous people I've ever known.

I sensed that when I gave "Cousin Ernie" his last haircut he knew the end was near. He rather philosophically spoke of how we can't take our money with us. And, I guess that's right. They don't put pockets in shrouds, nor do folks pull U-hauls behind hearses.

Our possessions, however, are not all that we leave behind. We leave a name.

In Cousin Ernie's case, he left a very good name.

BARBER-OSOPHY: When we have a good name, we'll be sorely missed by even our barber.

Quality, Not Quantity, Is What Counts in Life

Recently we began selling ice cream bars in the barbershop. For me that presents a real challenge. You see, my two favorite foods are ice cream and ice cream. So, I may eat up all my profit.

In spite of my dilemma, however, I was encouraged a bit when a customer told me of an interview he heard on television with a 100-year-old gentleman. When asked what he would do if he had it all to do over, the centenarian said, "I'd eat more ice cream." What a great philosophy!

Life is short, at best. So, we are bombarded with information (or misinformation) about health issues and how to prolong our lives. Some of the advice, however, reminds me of the fellow who was given six months to live. After getting over the initial shock, he told the doctor he decided to invite his mother-in-law to live with him. He said it wouldn't prolong his life, but it would make it *seem* longer.

While I certainly would not want to offend the medical profession (or my mother-in-law) or to encourage an unhealthy lifestyle, I have to wonder occasionally whether the quantity-of-life thing hasn't been a little overdone. After all, what good is quantity without quality?

Let me illustrate with what often happens during the end-of-year holiday season. It would be pretty safe to say that many experience at least a little guilt as they treat themselves to the wonderful foods of the season. Yet, if a person can't even enjoy holiday meals without feeling guilty, perhaps quantity of life has replaced quality.

As one who has never smoked cigarettes or participated in drinking alcoholic beverages, who exercises regularly and watches his weight, I still realize that tomorrow I could step off the curb and be hit by a bus.

Realizing the uncertainty and brevity of life, perhaps we ought to eat dessert first.

BARBER-OSOPHY: The person who always sacrifices quality of life for quantity may one day live to regret it.

THE TALE OF THREE BULLS

Regardless of the time of year, conversation in the barbershop often turns to football —mainly high school and college. In spite of my love of baseball, I still enjoy discussing San Antonio area football. I especially enjoy conversations concerning Alamo Heights and Judson football since the barbershop is in Alamo Heights and since my family is heavily involved at Judson.

Because of our involvement at Judson High School, I was invited some years ago to address the team prior to one of the playoff games. It was a great thrill, and I still enjoy the memory. I remember that I spoke on "Buying up Opportunities."

To illustrate my point, I told the story of the city boy who wanted to marry a farmer's daughter. The farmer didn't want to give up his daughter, so he told the boy he could marry the girl only if he (the boy) could catch and throw one of his three prize bulls. The boy agreed.

So, the farmer unleashed his first bull. It was big and mean, and the boy watched him as he ran past. The second bull was even worse, so the boy let that one pass, too.

The third bull, however, was the meanest of the bunch. But the city boy knew this was his last chance. He decided to grab the bull by the tail when he ran past. But when the boy reached out to grab its tail, he grabbed air instead. The bull had no tail, and the lad had missed his last opportunity to marry his sweetheart.

The application to opportunities in life and to the contest in which the athletes were about to engage was very obvious. I simply made the point that whatever the play was that unfolded in front of them, it might present the greatest opportunity they would have for a long time to show what they were made of. I added that the same is true of life.

Daily we are presented with opportunities to make a difference or to show what we are made of. What are we waiting for? A better opportunity? Remember the tale of three bulls!

BARBER-OSOPHY: Don't let any legitimate opportunities get away.

WHEN EXCEPTIONS RULE

I once heard a customer tell why he was glad he's no longer a schoolteacher. It was the usual negative stuff you hear about students these days.

I understood where he was coming from. Years ago I substitute taught for one day. That was enough for me to learn that most teachers are grossly underpaid.

Yet, I'm also familiar with the other side of the story. It involves those students who, years ago, were genuinely pulling for Sherry to pass her Excet Exam so that she could have a *permanent* teaching position at Judson High School. She also had students who stopped by her classroom to see how things were going with her mom on those critical days immediately after her mom's brain surgery. When I gave motivational lectures to high school freshmen, in appreciation, they all gave me I-like-you-because notes.

Unfortunately, these types of teenagers are not the ones who get most of the publicity. Generally, publicity is reserved for the negative exceptions.

This tendency of many of us to focus on the negative things in our society reminds me of an incident that occurred some years ago. It was the occasion on which one of our very fine citizens was murdered while transacting business at an automatic teller machine. This tragedy was discussed in the barbershop for days.

One of the reactions was rather interesting, however. It was as if some people immediately decided that ATM's were not safe. Although millions of people had safely used the machines, the publicity surrounding an isolated incident suddenly made their use to appear "high risk."

Actually, the headlines that should really concern us are not what we would normally expect. For instance, suppose the front-page headline read, "Man safely transacts business at ATM." Then we should certainly quit using them because, in that case, safety would have become the exception rather than the rule. Likewise, when the headline says, "Student gets to school and back home safely," that's when I'll suggest my wife quit teaching.

BARBER-OSOPHY: Beware of thinking negative exceptions are the rule.

The Cutting Edge

In

Sales and Service

BARBER-OSOPHY: "Good business
starts with good people."

No Vacancy

A young man who applied for a job was told there were no openings.

"What about Bill?" he asked. "Didn't he just quit?"

"He sure did," came the reply.

"Then have you already hired his replacement?" the young man asked.

"Nope."

"Then I'll fill that vacancy."

"You don't seem to understand," he was told. "Bill ain't left no vacancy."

Though funny, the story has a serious side. We would all like to think that, like George Bailey in *It's a Wonderful Life*, we would be missed by so many. We want to think that we are so indispensable that we could stick our finger in water, pull it out and leave a hole. But, how accurate is that assessment? It depends.

At work, it depends on our level of commitment. Too often you find those who are what I call L-I-F-O's. That stands for "last in" (the door for work) and "first out." For them, the job is just a job. They quit looking for work shortly after finding a job. And, because they feel no particular attachment to the company or the customers, were they to leave, they would hardly be missed.

On the other hand, there are those who feel a sense of mission or purpose. They are proud of the service they render and have a basic philosophy that says: When you do more than you're paid to do, someday (somewhere) you'll be paid more for what you do. Should they choose to take a job elsewhere, they would truly be missed.

Another application of our "vacancy principle" has to do with relationships. We all know certain people who will depart to even the sorrow of the undertaker. Others have "departed with no one's regret" (2 Chronicles 21:20).

This difference brings to mind two very different people. One is a customer whose wife continued to receive her traditional bouquet of flowers, even after he had passed. The florist was just doing what the devoted husband had instructed him to do every Monday.

Such loving kindness is in stark contrast to the fellow I overheard arguing with another gentleman in the checkout line. He thought that anyone who would buy his sweetheart something for Valentine's Day, as the gentleman had done, was a dope for being manipulated by the merchants and the media. Though I realize there are many ways to express love besides what is done on the one day, the man's attitude made me wonder if his sweetheart might hang out the "no vacancy" sign when he is gone.

BARBER-OSOPHY: How much we will be missed by our employer, our customers, our family or our friends depends largely upon our level of commitment.

COFFEE AND A TIP

One of the challenges of multi-career marriages is allotting time for the family and for each other. Some years ago, Sherry and I began to realize this and decided to take steps to insure "our time" every day. So, we began going to a convenient place in the evening just to have coffee and to visit.

We found it a bit amusing (and a compliment to our 35-year marriage) when some of the staff at one restaurant thought we were having an affair because we would often arrive in separate cars.

One of the places we enjoy coffee and dessert is the Menger Hotel. Not only is it a beautiful place, but also their coffee is some of the smoothest.

I remember one particular evening at the Menger. After our waiter brought our check and walked away with my $20, I commented to Sherry that I had forgotten to have him bring me plenty of one dollar bills. I knew that after the tip I would still need money for school lunches the next morning.

We decided to see if the waiter knew his stuff. If, on our $10 check, he brought back two fives or a ten dollar bill, we would know he was not on the ball. He did not disappoint us. He brought me plenty of ones and we, in turn, were generous with our tip.

Since a large part of a barber's income is from tips, I learned this lesson about making change a long time ago. Certainly, a person ought to get the same quality service whether he chooses to tip or not. That's a personal decision. But, if a person wants to tip, he shouldn't be inconvenienced by having to ask for change.

Along this line, I'm constantly amazed at how some folks in business never "get it" on this point. Whether it involves tipping, being seated, paying for services, or any other aspect of doing business, it needs to be easy, convenient and uncomplicated for the customer. The benefit to those in business is that we'll probably have more business and make more money.

But, there is another benefit. It is the satisfaction of knowing one is a true professional who treats others as he / she wants to be treated. Such an approach is almost irresistible in business, in relationships—and in marriages.

BARBER-OSOPHY: Always seek to make life a little easier for others.

A Buzz in the Parking Lot

A gentleman who was waiting for his haircut asked if I was going to charge the boy for the buzz I was giving. He laughed and said that if he had known that the boy simply wanted all his hair cut off, he could have done that for him in the parking lot—at no charge.

We took his comment as he intended and laughed good naturedly. Then I began thinking of some things I'd like to have asked the would-be barber.

First of all, since a buzz involves attaching a plastic clamp on the clippers and running it over the head, would he know which clamp to use for the proper cutting length?

Would the gentleman have been able to cut the sideburns the same length and outline around the ears, when he had finished cutting off all the boy's hair?

As a finishing touch, would he have been able to trim the hair across the forehead so that it was even, and then cut the hair at the base of the neck without nicking his customer?

Most likely, all of this could not have been done "in the parking lot." Don't forget, however, he *did* say he could cut it for free!

Yes, the customer was kidding, but there does seem to be an obvious point here, and it has to do with much more than just a haircut.

BARBER-OSOPHY: We usually get what we pay for—and very little for nothing.

CLEAR-HEADED BUSINESS PHILOSOPHY

I was thrilled to find a radio station that played country and western oldies. I switched stations on the shop radio, not because I don't like the old one but simply because I like the new one even better.

All was going well until customers began to notice what had happened. They liked the other station, and there was hardly a day that someone didn't comment to the effect that they *missed* the other station.

Their reaction put me to thinking of what would have been a parallel approach on my part regarding the radio. It's pretty obvious that I don't have any hair. That's kind of hard to hide. When speaking, I tell folks that when I began giving talks I realized the need for clarity of thought and expression. So, I asked the Lord to give me a clear head—and He did!

Also, my appearance is partly by choice. In other words, I'm decidedly clearheaded. One day I just decided I would have a clear head and began to shave what little hair there is around the sides.

Since my wife seems to like my hairstyle, I like it. This is probably true with most men. I could get into lots of trouble, however, by assuming because I like having no hair, all men like that style.

Yet, it seems that many businesses and salespeople make a similar mistake. The business owner assumes that the customer has the same likes and dislikes he or she has and sees no need to make any changes. Then they wonder why customers are turned off and don't come back. Often it's because customers found what *they* like elsewhere.

Everyone is ignorant about some things. Indeed, I may be ignorant about lots of things, but I ain't stupid. So, the dial on the radio went back where it was, and now I play what I prefer on the car radio and what my customers prefer in the barbershop.

BARBER-OSOPHY: A large part of business involves setting aside personal taste and prejudices in favor of what the customer likes, wants or needs.

CUSTOMER MELTDOWN

One morning, I attended the graveside service of a longtime customer of J.B.'s Barber Shop. While driving to the cemetery, I passed a certain restaurant and was reminded of an incident that happened there some years ago. Knowing the customer had a keen wit and sense of humor, I think he would have enjoyed this story. Maybe you will, too.

At the time the incident in the restaurant occurred, I was in direct sales. That particular day, I had a presentation a short distance from the establishment and decided to stop there for a cup of coffee, and go over my sales presentation.

When the waitress brought my coffee, I said to her, "Don't you think it's a bit warm in here?"

With a bit of a twang, she responded, "It sure is. We ain't got no air conditioning."

"How long has it been out?" I asked. Since it was the middle of the summer, I figured she would tell me it had been out a day or so.

You can imagine my surprise when she responded, "Ain't worked all summer."

"All summer?" I repeated. "That must have cost you some business."

The server's response is one I'll never forget: "Well, it has, but the owner feels like what he's lost in business he's made up in savings on the air conditioner."

Wow! You can't argue with that kind of logic. With that bit of penny-wise-pound-foolish philosophy, you wonder why the owner didn't run his business out of a tent and really cut back on overhead.

You also wonder what kind of mission statement goes with that approach. It seems it would have to be the kind that decorates the wall better than it guides the heart.

BARBER-OSOPHY: If the customer doesn't come first, don't be surprised when he doesn't come at all.

Who's Next?

The unthinkable happened. A customer got very angry. This is the unthinkable not because it doesn't happen in business, but because it is about the last thing you *want* to happen.

The customer got upset because, after he had waited about thirty minutes for his little boy to get in my chair, another customer cut in front of him. I can't say that I blame him for being furious. I think most people would have been upset.

What bothered me was not only that he was upset, but also that it was a situation over which I had little control. Yet, I felt responsible.

I have always tried to follow J.B.'s advice about who is next for a haircut: "When the shop is full, let the customers decide who is next. Otherwise, you can get yourself into a lot of trouble." But, generally, I know who is next and can, when the occasion requires, "make suggestions." But, this particular morning I had no idea who was next. They were all in their cars waiting for me when I unlocked the door. There was no way for me to know who drove up first.

After the man who cut in line jumped into my chair, I could tell by the demeanor of the dad what had happened. Then it became a question of how to handle the situation. Should I have the man get out of the chair and risk a scene? Should I risk embarrassing him? The best solution seemed to be for me to give him a fast haircut, take his money and thank him for coming in. I then turned my attention to the man who had already put his boy in my chair.

Clearly, the problem was the fault of the man who had just walked out the door. He should have been the one apologizing. He should have been dealing with what the dad was saying about the incident. Yet, considered from another point of view (1) I own the business, (2) I am responsible for what happens in my business, (3) I felt badly for what I allowed to happen and (4) it didn't cost anything to sincerely apologize to the dad – both before and after his boy's haircut.

BARBER-OSOPHY: If you are not responsible for what takes place in your business, who is?

THE UNAPPRECIATED CUSTOMER

Suppose a customer asks, "How much do you get for a haircut?"

"Twenty dollars for a haircut and shampoo," I reply.

"But, I don't want a shampoo. All I want is a haircut. How much is it for just a haircut?"

"Sorry, we have a new policy," I answer. "Haircut and shampoo or nothing."

How long do you suppose we would stay in business with such nonsense? Yet, we are all exposed to this approach with increasing frequency.

Recently I was told at a restaurant that the entrée I was accustomed to ordering was only available at about three times the size and twice the price. When I told a manager that I saw no need to buy more than I (or Bexar county) could consume and that I thought it would be a waste of food and money, his response was essentially, "Too bad." Who cares that what they had been serving was enormously popular? Suddenly, the consumer became unimportant, and the bottom line became the guiding principle.

Such disregard for what the customer wants and likes is similar to a fictitious story about the fellow who walked into the hardware store and asked for his usual supply of red widgets. The person at the counter told him they didn't carry them anymore. When the customer asked why, he was told, "Because when we did, we couldn't keep them in stock."

A fellow speaker* tells the story of how he wanted a particular type of promotional cup that was being offered at his favorite fast food restaurant. In the ad it was offered with a type of soda he didn't care for. But, he felt that was okay as long as he got one of those cups. When he ordered, the lady asked, "And what type of soda would you like in that cup?"

"You mean I have a choice?" he asked.

"Sir," she said, "this is America, and in America you always have a choice."

This choice includes the choice of who gets our business.

BARBER-OSOPHY: When those in business consistently help customers in their choice to do business elsewhere, the business has no right to complain when it goes broke.

---

* Taken from a presentation by Larry Wingate.

COMMON SENSE BUSINESS DEBTS

Sometimes, after a customer gets out of the chair, he will ask, "What do I owe you?" It's certainly a reasonable question, since we are in business to make a profit.

For those of us in business, however, the question should often be reversed: What does the business owe the customer? If we want to succeed, certain obligations must be met. So, let's look at a few common sense "business debts" that are easily overlooked.

BUSINESS OWES THE CUSTOMER:

1. A comfortable, relaxed environment. While this may not be what everyone expects from every business, it's generally the case. Thus, I'm always puzzled as to why customers must be cooked or frozen while having to listen to music that would drive a person to drink. Who are we are trying to please—the staff or the customers?

2. A smile. This doesn't mean a person has to always look like he ate a banana sideways. But, it does mean that no one likes to do business with someone who looks like he was weaned on a dill pickle. A pleasant disposition costs so little and means so much—to us and to others.

3. What he wants. This involves listening skills to determine what the customer wants. The customer doesn't always want or like the same things as the person in business. For instance, (as per a previous chapter) just imagine what all the customers who come out of J.B.'s would look like if I assumed everyone wanted their haircut like mine. Owners of successful businesses listen in order to determine what the customers want, as opposed to simply selling what we think he (she) ought to have.

4. *Common sense.* Often we get customers who want to talk. Common sense says we listen. On the other hand, if a customer gets in the chair and opens a magazine, common sense says he doesn't want conversation. Similarly, if a guest is sitting in a restaurant with his/her sweetheart, engaged in an intimate conversation, what should this tell the server about repeated or lengthy interruptions? You can think of similar applications for your business.

5. *Trust.* This means that we can be trusted to deliver a good product at a fair price, and that we can be trusted not to gossip or to betray a confidence.

How do you and your business measure up? How do we at J.B.'s measure up? Speaking only for myself, I'd have to say that I do better on some things than others. If we want customers to continue asking "What do I owe you?," we had better keep asking the same question of our customers.

BARBER-OSOPHY: Business often reaps what is owes.

Three Requirements for Attracting and Keeping Good People

Mark Twain said that he felt he could live a whole month on one good compliment. How about you, or the folks who work for you?

Not long ago, as I was working and chatting with customers, I received what I thought was one of the nicest compliments a person in business can receive. The compliment was to the effect that I was having such a good time with customers that I ought to pay them instead of them paying me. The observation reminded me of a couple of things.

First is the obvious. If the COMPLIMENT made me feel good, wouldn't a compliment make the other person feel the same way? If that's the case, why don't I compliment other people more often?

I'm afraid that too often, rather than finding something positive to say, I tend to find fault as if there is a reward for doing so. If you're susceptible to the same tendency, perhaps you should remember that no monument has ever been built to a professional critic. Yet, teamwork is often built around compliments, encouragement and positive words.

The second thing that the customer's comment brings to mind is how appealing a POSITIVE ATTITUDE and having a good time are to others. No one wants to be around a sour puss. We all would prefer to be associated with (and do business with) folks who look like they just walked through a revolving door on someone else's push.

This principle not only applies to customers but to employees as well. When it comes to retaining staff, the feeling of having a good time while working goes a long way. One of the strongest recruiting tools is word of mouth. A powerful means of recruiting results when a staff member tells a friend in the business: "You need to come work where I work. It is such a fun, positive environment."

Yet, there is more to reducing turnover and recruiting than just having a good time and paying compliments, though these things are important. The MAIN THING is also important.

Someone has said that *the main thing in business is to keep the main thing the main thing.* Yet, what is the *main thing*? Every time I ask this question, something that happened some years ago comes to mind.

I had a morning presentation in Corpus Christi and I took my wife and son along. After staying overnight in a hotel, I got up early the morning of the presentation and went down to the restaurant, intending to let Sherry and Jon sleep a bit longer while I had coffee and read.

When the waitress came over to take my order, I simply asked for coffee and a Danish. She then asked what kind of Danish.

"Do you have a cheese Danish?" I asked.

She then said something I'll never forget: "I'll go see. But, management doesn't like for us to tell people when we have cheese Danish because, when we tell them, we sell out too fast."

Well, she found a cheese Danish! She approached my table with such satisfaction you would have thought she was bringing me the Hope Diamond on a saucer.

I tell this to make a point in regard to the *main thing* in business. Do you think this restaurant had lost sight of the main thing? Do you think we sometimes do the same thing?

The *main thing* in business is to make money—even if you have to order more Danish, so to speak. Of nearly equal value as the *main thing* are satisfied customers—since we won't make money for long without customers. All else is secondary.

Too often we, as business owners or managers, become so caught up in paper work, crisis management, majoring in minors and nitpicking that we get in the way of our staff pleasing customers and making money—for themselves and for us. Then, before we know it, we are searching for a new employee. And, if we are not careful, we eventually earn a reputation with customers and potential employees as being too negative to be around, short sighted when it comes to running a business and petty in our dealings with others.

While many factors enter into the success or failure of any business, staffing has to be at the top of the list. If one were to ask why some succeed in this important area while others fail, the answer might be closer than is realized.

BARBER-OSOPHY: Good people build good businesses.

GROWTH

STIMULATORS

BARBER-OSOPHY: "Few things are more dangerous than a ten-year-old mind in a fully-developed body."

THE UPSIDE-DOWN TREE

In a large clay pot in one corner of J.B.'s Barber Shop sat a Norfolk pine. A longtime customer gave it to us many years ago. Until the pine died several years ago, it was quite a conversation piece.

One of the unusual things about the Norfork pine is that it is not a pine at all. It's actually a fern.

Our customers pointed out from time to time that our tree was larger at the top than at the bottom, giving it the appearance of being upside down.

It didn't always have that shape. It took that shape after I moved it from the front window to the back of the shop and placed a chair on one side of it and a soda machine on the other.

J.B.'s theory was that the tree didn't grow as much at the bottom as the top because of the objects on either side close to the bottom. It makes sense.

In a similar way, environment and associations often affect us. For example, when Texans move to the north, it's just a matter of time before they start speaking with an accent. Conversely, when a Northerner moves to Texas, in no time at all we have the person speaking normally.

Jesting aside, Andrew Carnegie was once asked how he accounted for the fact that he had more than forty millionaires working for him. He responded that they weren't millionaires when they started with him. Evidently the Carnegie environment shaped their thinking.

The Indians have a saying: "The boy who runs with the dogs learns to bark." I guess that's all right for those who want to bark.

But, for those who don't want to bark (complain, criticize, or habitually entertain negative thoughts), there's an important lesson here.

BARBER-OSOPHY: If you don't like the direction in which you're growing, change your environment.

"It's a Churchill Thing"

When our daughters were in the Judson band, we would often go to marching contests. One of the things that I remember about the events was the competitive spirit between the Judson band and the crosstown Winston Churchill High School band. It seems this competitive spirit was heightened by a slogan that appeared on T-shirts displayed by Churchill band members when they were not performing on the field. It read: "It's a Churchill Thing."

Recently I've been telling customers about another "Churchill Thing" of which I was the recipient at a recent basketball game between Churchill and Judson.

Sherry and I arrived late at Littleton Gym where the game was to be played. She located a couple of seats for us while I purchased something to eat.

As I walked in front of the Churchill fans, I dropped an order of nachos. Splat! It was not one of my finest moments. But, I just kept walking and didn't even look up.

Like the fellow who has a mouthful of hot coffee, I figured whatever I did next was not going to be good. But, I managed to get across the gym with the rest of my order and with a semblance of dignity.

As Sherry and I were munching on the remaining order of nachos, two Churchill cheerleaders appeared in front of me holding another order. They said they saw what had happened and felt badly about it. So, they wanted to replace the order of nachos I'd dropped!

I was stunned. I thought it was one of the sweetest things I'd ever seen, and I told them so. After they walked away, Sherry read my mind. "I wonder if they know you're going to write about them?"

"I guess they will when I send them a copy!" I replied.

BARBER-OSOPHY: One of the best forms of class is the kind that is easily touched by the misfortune of another.

Livin' on "Someday I'll"

One of the nice things about our 48-year-old barbershop is that we get to see customers go through the various stages of life. In some cases, we even give first haircuts to those whose grandfathers got their first haircuts at J.B.'s.

It's quite interesting to watch the little fellows as they become accustomed to the new experience. Generally, we find they get more worked up over the second haircut than they do the first. Yet, after they settle into the routine, they start looking forward to playing with the toys and to receiving gum or a lollipop after their haircut. Then they simply display the happy, carefree disposition of little boys. They don't worry about being happy. They're just happy! At this stage of their lives, the hokey pokey is pretty much what it's all about.

As these little boys become teenagers, their upbeat attitude often changes. Some of them become infected with the same attitude that plagues most adults. It's an attitude that postpones happiness through a "someday I'll…" approach.

With such a mindset, a person feels that happiness will come someday when certain conditions are met. The boy (or girl) may feel that happiness will occur when he graduates from high school. Then the thought changes to, "When I go off to college." In college he wishes he could get through and get on with life. Then he realizes that, for happiness, he needs a JOB to go with his Ph.D. Following that, he would be happy if he could just get married, have children, own a business, get out of debt, retire or travel. Someday, everything will be great!

Stephen Leacock, the Canadian humorist, said it very well: "Life, we learn too late, is in the living, in the tissue of every day and every hour."

Dr. Maxwell Maltz, author of *Psycho-Cybernetics*,* observed that, once the mind accepts the concept of conditional happiness, one will never be happy. Once that requirement is met, the mind, being so conditioned, will immediately go to work to set up the next prerequisite for happiness. Thus, an endless, futile cycle.

Maltz concluded that if, a person is going to be happy, it will never be because of something. It will always be—*period*! So, maybe there's more to the hokey pokey philosophy than we thought.

BARBER-OSOPHY: Mature people have a childlike, happy disposition.

---

*Dr. Maxwell Maltz, Ph.D., F.I.C.S., *Psycho-Cybernetics*, 1988 Audio Renaissance Tapes, Inc., 9110 Sunset Blvd., Suite 200, Los Angeles, CA. 90069

WHEN THE ZEROES DON'T ADD UP

I had been sitting at the computer working on a column for a local paper when the phone rang. I jumped like someone had poked me in the ribs. After I got over the shock, however, I was glad to hear the lady's voice on the other end. We had been trying to work out details on a presentation for her group, and we had been playing phone tag.

After arrangements were set for the speech, she asked about purchasing books for her group. I told her the books were $10 each and that I would bring them to the meeting. I also told her that for the 150 that would be in attendance the total cost of the books would be $150. She said that sounded great and to just fax over an invoice.

Shortly after I said "bye," it hit me. "I just agreed to sell my books for $1 a piece instead of $10. I just lost $1350 on 150 books. I must be twins. No one person can be so dumb."

Actually, it was the type of mistake anyone could make. It was the result of not focusing on the matter at hand. Part of the brain was still on the column. Once I realized what I had done, the miscalculation had my undivided attention! It also taught me a valuable lesson. Being a math teacher, Sherry would say the lesson should be to use a calculator instead of doing math in my head. I would say I learned to completely shift gears before turning to the next matter of business.

Here are some additional life lessons the incident brought to mind:

1. When a person makes a mistake, the best approach is to admit it quickly and emphatically.

Though once again I got the answering machine, I said, "What I've done is so dumb, you're not going to believe it. You're about to find out that I'm a much better speaker than I am a mathematician."

2. A problem well stated is half solved.

"When I gave you the total price, I figured for 15 books instead of 150."

3. There is no substitute for integrity.

"Because of my error, I'll be happy to give you the books at half price. Or, if that is not acceptable, I'll do whatever is right." (Even if it means losing $1350.)

4. If a real good batter in the major leagues only gets a hit one out of every three times at the plate, why should we expect a higher batting average in life?

We're going to make some mistakes that end up costing us in dollars or costing us other ways. But, what choice do we have? Do *nothing*? That only leads to achieving nothing—or worse—*being* nothing. It's far better to accept that we all make mistakes and then to learn from our mistakes.

BARBER-OSOPHY: Mistakes often wake us up and make us grow.

Painful Lessons

Many of our customers wish to shake the barber's hand before getting in the chair. I like that most of the time. The time when I was a bit apprehensive about it was when my ring finger on the right hand was healing from a volleyball sprain.

At first it was so painful to shake hands I would just offer the left hand and an explanation. As with most explanations, that soon got old. Rather than having to explain and sounding like a complainer, I soon adopted an alternative: (1) Slide the hand completely into the other person's hand so that the sore finger is not wedged between the other fingers and (2) keep the hand firm. In other words, concentrate! Otherwise, I could wind up on my knees.

Actually, the minor injury was a learning experience. First of all, I learned how careless I had become with my handshake, and secondly how painful a lapse in concentration could be.

I also learned a little more about the way others shake hands. I noticed especially the difference between firm and vice-like. It was probably the only time a cold-fish handshake could actually be appreciated.

But, the experience provided a third lesson. This one relates to asking too many questions regarding obvious injuries or surgeries. To have to answer such questions over and over can get a little trying. Yet, it's nice that people care enough to ask in the first place.

BARBER-OSOPHY: Painful lessons are often the ones that stick with us the longest.

Advice Can Be Fishy

Some years ago while Jon was shining shoes in the shop, a customer was giving him business advice. Since the man is retired from a rather successful business, I was pleased that Jon listened. The conversation, however, reminded me of how easy it is to take too much advice.

I heard of a man who opened a fish market but was having little success. A friend stopped in and asked how things were going.

"Not well," the entrepreneur replied.

"Well, I can understand that," the friend said. "You don't even have a sign advertising your business. How do you expect to get customers if they don't even know you're here? Get a sign."

This seemed like good advise. So the merchant hung up a big sign: FRESH FISH SOLD HERE TODAY.

After a while, business improved. Then someone walked in and said, "I've been wondering why you have TODAY on your sign. Obviously, it's today and not tomorrow." So, the man decided that the customer was right and painted over "today."

Before long, someone else came in and said that the word FRESH seemed unnecessary, since obviously he, being a man of integrity, wouldn't sell old fish. So, off came "fresh."

Next, someone said the words SOLD HERE seemed unnecessary, since it was obvious he wasn't in business somewhere else.

So, all that remained was FISH.

Then in walked a customer and announced, "I smelled your fish three blocks away. Isn't that advertising enough?"

So, that was the end of the sign.

Several months later, the man was bemoaning his business woes. "Well, what do you expect?" a friend remarked. "You don't even have a sign!"

BARBER-OSOPHY: Most successful people have a knack for knowing who to listen to.

Teacher, Teacher, I Declare

We often see businesses with signs that say: "No shoes, no shirt, no service."

I'm thankful that I have the type of customers for whom such a sign is not necessary. That does not change the fact that inappropriate dress is becoming increasingly prevalent.

Sometimes I wonder if underwear might have been misnamed. One would naturally think that the term refers to garments that are to be worn under other clothes. But, it seems more and more people think otherwise.

One day as Sherry and I were having coffee at a place near our home, in walked a young man in his undershirt. It was not even a T-shirt, but rather what teenagers call "a wife beater."

The teen walked up to the counter and asked to speak to his friend who worked in the back. When his friend appeared, the teen asked him if they were still hiring.

I don't know what he was told, but Sherry and I found it amusing (and pathetic) that he would even consider looking for a job dressed in such a manner. As it turned out, we had misjudged the situation.

As the young man walked out of the restaurant and started to get in his car, he began peeling off his undershirt. Actually, I guess he had dressed up for the occasion and was simply taking off his equivalent of a tie.

How sad that some have no sense of class, decency or respect. On the other hand, it's refreshing to have a part in grooming folks who take pride in their appearance.

BARBER-OSOPHY: People with class dress for the occasion, or they don't go.

I Confess—
I Slipped in Under the Fence

Some time ago, Jon and Sherry were out of town for the week. I jokingly told folks I was running things in the Sumerlin house. I was running the washer, the dryer, the microwave and other appliances.

I was also having a wild time. One night I stayed up till eleven. Another night, I took my mom to the IMAX for her birthday. Oh yes, and there was the night I went to church. But, the real wild time was had at a Little League game.

It all began when a customer who coached the Alamo Heights all-star team told me of a game they were going to play at O.P. Schnabel Park. I thought, "Alright! I love baseball, and it sure beats sitting at home in an empty house. Besides, I know many of the parents and kids who are involved."

So, on the day of the game, I left directly from J.B.'s so that there would be plenty of time to get across town for the 7 P.M. game. As it turned out, I arrived in plenty of time—with over an hour to spare. With book in hand, I entered the park, found a picnic table and began to read.

Before long I found the answer to eating my own cooking and purchased six or seven buck's worth of "health food" at the concession stand. Having dined like a king, I was ready for baseball.

As the game progressed, I began to stroll around and visit with friends. Suddenly, a league "official" (which league is unimportant) walked up and asked, "Sir, would you like to buy an admission ticket?" At first, I didn't know what he was talking about. Then I asked, "How much is it?" Next thing I knew, I had swapped a dollar for a small ticket and a very satisfied "official."

I had also traded my dollar for a story that still makes me laugh. After all, not many people can attract surveillance at a Little League game. Yet, apparently, someone had seen me come in and had tracked me for about two hours. Whoever did that must have seen me invest a fortune in eats. But, that didn't matter. A rule had been broken, and the "official's" job is to enforce rules. Otherwise, his authority and importance are diminished. Ah yes, and there's the rub with authority—that feeling of importance.

BARBER-OSOPHY: Where rules and ego are present, common sense is absent.

RIVER RAMBLINGS

I was born in the Nix Hospital right here in San Antonio, and though we have made our home here for the past fifteen years, I never tire of the downtown area. I especially enjoy the Riverwalk.

Since the barbershop is closed on Monday mornings, often I will grab a good book and head downtown. After reading for a while, I take what's left of my coffee and walk along the river. It's so relaxing! It's a stimulant to the creative juices.

Sometimes while walking, I try to imagine what it would be like to be a tourist taking such a stroll for the first time. Have you ever noticed how much more we enjoy sights and sounds while on vacation? I try to enjoy the Riverwalk as if I'm on a mini-vacation seeing the sights for the first time.

I sometimes notice that not all vacationers on the river seem to be having a good time. They often look like they were weaned on a dill pickle. In fact, were it not for their tourist dress and appurtenances, you would never guess by their expressions that they're on vacation. If they're having a good time, they surely forgot to tell their faces.

But, why should this surprise me? I've seen the same expressions on cruises. Believe it or not, some people can be in the lap of luxury, seemingly without a care in the world, and have a permanent scowl. I once saw passengers boo a crew member because disembarkation at one port was not to their satisfaction. It made me wonder why they chose to spend their time and money to go half way around the world to be unhappy. They could have stayed home and been miserable for nothing.

This serves to illustrate a simple concept: We have within us the ability to enjoy daily mini-vacations or to be miserable on trips of a lifetime.

BARBER-OSOPHY: Where you are isn't as important as the fact that *you* are there.

An All-too-Common Addiction

It was a beautiful spring morning in LaJolla, California . I had flown to San Diego the evening before. After a pleasant breakfast, the cab driver had taken me five miles to LaJolla. In an hour and a half he was to pick me up for the trip to the San Diego airport, where I would catch a shuttle for the two-hour trip down to Ensanada, Mexico. From there I would board the *Dawn Princess* to Hawaii.

As I strolled through LaJolla, I was completely charmed by its gorgeous Pacific setting and its quaint shops. I sat in one of the shops and sipped coffee while reading a book and looking at the ocean.

As it got closer to time for Ebbie, the cab driver, to pick me up, I started walking back to LaJolla Cove, where we were to meet. Passing through Ellen Browning Scripps Park, I noticed joggers, walkers, lovers and sightseers. I walked up to a rail and joined the sightseers and stood speechless while gazing at the grandeur of breakers against the rocky shoreline.

A hundred yards or so below was a middle-aged couple sitting on a rock. It appeared they, too, were enjoying the sights, as well as each other's company.

Suddenly, I couldn't believe my eyes! "You've got to be kidding," I thought. "That lady is actually talking on a cell phone." In one of the most beautiful and romantic places in the world, while apparently with her husband, she was on her cell phone. If I had been her husband, I would have been sorely tempted to push her into the water.

As I turned to walk to the spot where Ebbie would be waiting, I spotted a bag lady who was walking around in the park talking to herself. I couldn't help thinking she had more sense than the lady on the cell phone.

What is it with people and cell phones? I admit to being biased on the subject. After all, I've not only had to stop cutting hair so customers could answer trivial calls, I've also had someone who was seated on the front row talk on his phone during one of my speeches. So, I have some rather strong feelings about rude people and their phones. I understand that the devices serve a vital purpose when used wisely. What I don't understand is why they have become as important to the average person as an oxygen bottle to a respiratory patient.

I also don't understand why at nearly every restaurant there is someone with a cell phone talking loud enough to be heard in three counties. Is it to impress folks with the fact he/she has a phone? It's really not that big a deal. Some underprivileged school kids also have them.

And, what ever happened to private conversations? I long for the days when people went into phone booths —*and closed the door.* Is there no sense of privacy anymore? Who wants to overhear conversations about private business deals or someone's love life?

For five straight days, while the *Dawn Princess* was at sea, we were out of range for cell phones. It was wonderful. The moment we made land, like smokers starved for nicotine, many began to dial frantically. I began looking for a "no phoning section."

BARBER-OSOPHY: Somewhat like money, electronic devices make wonderful servants and lousy masters.

Vote Against Indifference

Someone has jokingly said that in a recent poll when voters were asked which they thought was a bigger problem in America—ignorance or indifference, one respondent said he didn't know and didn't care

At J.B.'s Barber Shop, customers are definitely not indifferent when presidential elections come around. Understandably, elections create lots of conversation.

I can't understand the person who doesn't even care enough to vote in the various elections. This I find very disturbing.

I'm always tempted to tell such indifferent people about how, as a sailor during World War II, my dad was on the aircraft carrier the *USS Saratoga*, which was hit several times by enemy fire and suicide pilots. I'd like to share with them that when I was a small boy, we had to leave the drive-in movie because the war story that was showing had my dad so upset. It was one of the few times I ever saw him cry. More than a half-century later, he sometimes had nightmares about the horrors of war.

He's certainly not the only one of whom such things could be said. In the history of this country, hundreds of thousands have suffered and died for the freedoms we enjoy—including the freedom to vote. Yet, if indifference toward these freedoms continues to grow as it has, I wonder how long we will be able to enjoy such freedoms.

Often indifference is excused by saying, "I don't get involved in politics." As citizens, however, we *are* involved whether we want to be or not. The frightening thing is how this I-don't want- to-get-involved attitude strikes at the very roots of freedom.

I was reminded of this lesson some years ago while visiting the New England Holocaust Memorial. It is located in the heart of Boston near the Freedom Trail. The memorial was dedicated on October 21, 1995, about a week before my visit.

The memorial consists of luminous glass towers, each 54-feet high. The six towers recall the six main death camps. The six million numbers that are etched in orderly fashion on the glass remind us of the infamous tattooed numbers and the ledgers of the Nazi bureaucracy.

As one walks through the memorial, quotes from survivors and informative texts can be read at various points. Regardless of the number of visitors, the silence at the memorial is deafening.

At the end of the path, which winds through the towers, stands a large black granite panel bearing the legendary words of the Lutheran minister, Martin Niemoeller. These moving words were etched into the panel:

THEY CAME FIRST for the Communist,
and I didn't speak up because I wasn't a Communist.

THEN THEY CAME for the Jews,
and I didn't speak up because I wasn't a Jew.

THEN THEY CAME for the trade unionists,
and I didn't speak up because I wasn't a trade unionist.

THEN THEY CAME for the Catholics,
and I didn't speak up because I was a Protestant.

THEN THEY CAME for me,
and by that time no one was left to speak up.*

BARBER-OSOPHY: The price of being free is involvement.

---

*Facts are taken from materials provided by the New England Holocaust Memorial.

GETTING PERSONAL ABOUT COMMITMENT

Henrietta the hen and Pattie the pig went for a stroll in the forest. They came upon a hapless stranger who was tired, hungry and lost. Henrietta came up with an idea: They would provide a breakfast for the stranger. Henrietta would supply the eggs and Pattie would provide the bacon.

When the hen made the suggestion to Pattie, the pig first thought it was a good idea. Then it dawned on her, and she squealed, "For you that's a small sacrifice, but for me that represents total commitment."

I must confess that after 9-11 I felt a bit like Henrietta the hen. With respect to the sacrifices that so many made involving tremendous acts of kindness and service, and even the sacrifice of life, my small sacrifices paled in significance.

I tried to find a flag to hang at the shop. I refused to take money for a haircut from an EMT and, instead, shook his hand and told him how greatly I appreciate what he does every day. I prayed often for those who lost loved ones, for our leaders and for our country. Yet, what real sacrifices did I make?

I didn't know what else to do, but still yearned to do more. Maybe you shared the same feelings.

There is a certain dilemma in such feelings of admiration for those who are directly involved. It is much like the folks who saw the man walk a tightrope across Niagara Falls. After he had made several trips across and back, the crowd went wild with admiration. When the applause died down, he turned and asked for a show of hands on how many would like to see him push a wheelbarrow across. All hands shot up. Suddenly he said, "Okay, someone climb in and let's go." There was not a single volunteer.

It seems that every day I heard someone talk of what "we" ought to do. Such is natural. Something must be done! No question about it. Yet, "we" don't have to make the tough decisions, nor lay down our lives. Generally speaking, others do those things for us.

Though we can and should be supportive of those who are directly involved in the process, it appears that we should also be careful about glibly committing others to sacrifices we either have not made or would not be willing to make in one form or another. There is a type of hypocrisy in "commitment" without the "me."

BARBER-OSOPHY: Commitment involves a personal willingness to make whatever sacrifices are necessary.

WHEN

THINGS

GET HAIRY

BARBER-OSOPHY: "Stress is an inside thing.
A simple cure is reaching outward."

The Sunrise of a New Day

"This is why we live in South Texas." We hear those, or similar words, on so many beautiful days.

It may be true that our summers can be tough, but South Texas spring and fall are hard to beat. And, the mornings are absolutely incredible.

Benjamin Franklin said, "The morning has gold in its mouth." Milton said, "Sweet is the breath of morn..." To see the first rays of light, as the horizon turns purple in the east, and then to see the colors change from orange to red before the sun completely bursts forth, is to me one of life's most precious moments. I love sunrises!

I also love the feeling of seizing the opportunity that comes from being "up and at um" when the day begins. I don't believe in burning daylight, and I strongly believe the early bird gets the worm. My house has always had a few occupants who disagreed, however, and who had no interest at all in worms. Nevertheless, I do my best thinking and my best work with the rising of the sun.

I also find that morning is a time of hope. If, as Vince Lombardi said, "Fatigue makes cowards of us all"— rest and a new day often give us courage. A new day also gives hope. Surely, as long as the sun continues to rise, nothing is hopeless.

In keeping with these thoughts, there is a beautiful poem written by the famous Indian dramatist, Kalidasa, c. 500. It's called "Salutation to the Dawn."

> Look to this day!
> For it is life, the very life of life.
> In its brief course
> Lie all the verities and realities of your existence:
> > The bliss of growth
> > The glory of action
> > The splendor of beauty,
> For yesterday is but a dream
> And tomorrow is only a vision,
> But today well lived makes every yesterday a dream
> > of happiness
> And every tomorrow a vision of hope.
> Look well, therefore, to this day!
> Such is the salutation to the dawn.

BARBER-OSOPHY: Those who aren't thankful for today will likely waste tomorrow.

ONE AT A TIME

Saturdays at J.B's are notoriously busy. It's not unusual for every waiting chair to be taken. It's a dream come true for any business.

During such times it can become very noisy and the pace can get a bit frantic. As a barber, you can get so tired and uptight that before the day is over, you have to remind yourself that it is a dream and not a nightmare.

Since our schedule is such that I'm alone for the first three hours on Friday mornings, the same situation sometimes occurs for me. Believe me, those three hours can get a bit hairy (pun intended). The shop fills up, and I'm it.

During such times, I sometimes tell myself, "You can just work on one customer at a time. It makes no difference how many are in the shop; it still comes down to one at a time."

Recently, though, this approach took a different turn. It was a Friday morning, and I was alone with only the customer on whom I was working.

"Where are all your customers?" he asked.

"You know it's real strange. I've been busy all morning with one in and one out. And you know, I can just work on one at a time anyway."

"Well, that's right," he chuckled.

But, it's right about more than just haircuts. It's right about life.

How often do we get stressed and upset when our in-basket gets too full? Yet, no matter how much we have to do, each task must be done one at a time. In much the same way that there will be people who need haircuts when I'm dead and gone, our in-basket will not be empty at that time either.

Then there is the other side of the coin. We get anxious about the future before we even finish the present. We start worrying about customers who haven't even arrived.

BARBER-OSOPHY: We can cut only one head of hair at a time.

THE DOOR TO HAPPINESS

One Saturday morning, I looked out the front of the barbershop just in time to see the odd way a customer was parking. There was only one other car in front of the shop. Yet, this gentleman parked so close to the other car there was no way the owner would ever be able to get in from the driver's side.

It reminded me of the time I accidentally did a similar thing and came out to find a very nasty note on my windshield. Since this situation was none of my concern, I made no comment about it when the gentleman came into the shop and sat down for his haircut. But, I did wonder what was going to happen when the other customer left to get in his car.

It was not a big deal. He simply walked to his car, sized up the situation and very calmly climbed in on the passenger side. Then he slid behind the wheel.

In a little while, the fellow who had parked so close took his new haircut, got in his car and drove off—completely oblivious to what he had done. I'm sure it was unintentional.

After both fellows were gone, I commented to J.B. on what had just happened. Since he was standing outside when the gentleman was forced to get into his car from the passenger side, he provided an interesting detail to what had happened. He said the fellow simply remarked, "Oh, well, I might do the same thing some-day." Wow!

How often do you suppose this fellow has a bad day? We might also wonder about his blood pressure and his relationships. They're probably all in pretty good shape.

Though our story is short and not very profound, it illustrates a profound principle.

BARBER-OSOPHY: People and circumstances make us neither happy nor unhappy. We choose such attitudes.

A Terminal Connection

As we sat on the runway at Dallas-Fort Worth Airport waiting our turn to take off, I stared out the window. The two hours to get from Miami International Airport to the port where I would board ship lessened by the minute.

I kept thinking how much easier it would be to catch the ship *before* it left the dock.

The dignified, middle-aged lady sitting next to me was also stressed. When I asked, "How are you?" her answer had clearly indicated it was not a red-letter day and that she wished to be left alone. So, we sat in silence.

When we were finally in the air with time to spare on my two-hour window, we both began to relax. The lady told me that she was employed by the state of Louisiana, traveled abroad extensively, was fluent in French and once taught English in Europe. She was fascinating!

When she asked what I do, I told her I'm a Barber-osopher and was taking a cruise out of Miami in order to give a seminar aboard ship. I was astounded to find that she didn't know what a Barber-osopher is!

For over an hour, we talked, laughed, shared, and enjoyed. In no time we landed.

Before landing, she remarked that she felt much better than when she boarded. We said "goodbye" and "let's stay in touch."

She walked off the plane about five minutes ahead of me, and I got off looking for my daughter who was to accompany me on the cruise. To my surprise, just inside the terminal was my one-time distant, stressed friend. She said she just wanted to tell me to have a great trip.

It has been said that no one is useless in this world when he or she lightens the burden of someone else.

BARBER-OSOPHY: Stress is an inside thing. A simple cure is reaching outward.

THOSE BOILS ON THE NECK

I hate painting. I hate the preparation. I hate wondering if the paint is covering evenly. I hate dripping paint everywhere. And, I hate the cleanup.

However, I figure I'm not alone. As the weather gets warmer and folks begin doing things the weather has not permitted them to do, some folks will be outdoors—painting. Though I don't have any helpful hints on how to do a better or faster job, maybe the following story about a paint job will help us improve our attitude about life.

A few years ago, one of my summer jobs included applying a coat of paint in the barbershop. You would think that the way I hate painting I would have just hired a painter. Even if I had been willing to part with the cash, it would have been a bit embarrassing to have someone paint a spot the size of a door. That's right—the size of a door.

The reason for the small job was that our neighbors in the business next door decided they wanted to close in a door on the wall between the barbershop and their business. After asking if it was okay with me, they removed the door and dry-walled the area. All I had to do was prepare the surface, paint it and hang a bulletin board in the space. It wasn't a big deal. It wasn't like I had to paint the Empire State Building with a water-color brush. Yet, Sherry would say that is the way I acted.

I'm ashamed to say that though the job actually only took about three hours, for days I whined, complained and procrastinated. Sherry listened while I made a mountain out of a molehill and wound up acting pretty silly and rather immature. Ever done such a thing?

This approach toward little things reminds me of something Samuel Pepys recorded in his *Diary*. He tells of witnessing the execution of Sir Harry Van. He was beheaded, by the way. As Sir Harry Van mounted the platform, he was pleading with the executioner. Not for his life—understand! He was pleading with the executioner not to strike the painful boil on the back of his neck.

BARBER-OSOPHY: Many that bravely endure the "executions of life" are turned into whiners by mere "boils on the neck."

J.B.'s Barber Shop and Sauna

When the air conditioning quit working in Sherry's car, I should have known it was going to be a weekend to forget. After all, that's not a good sign considering our August heat.

Yet, all seemed to be going reasonably well. Church on Sunday and lunch at mom's on Monday were both very nice.

Then the wheels came off. We had a run-in with one of Sherry's students—he rear-ended us! The next five hours were spent at the accident scene and in the hospital emergency room. Fortunately, we didn't seem to have any injuries. Just aches and pains. While in ER, however, I developed hives over much of my body. (Probably nerves.) I had itching to contend with after I went to bed.

But that's not all. The next morning before leaving for the shop, I stopped by the office to get the e-mails. I had two from the same friend. When I clicked on the second message, it told me not to open the first one, because it contained a virus. Oops! Too late!

When I arrived at the shop, I discovered the air conditioning was out. Our customers and staff spent the morning in a sauna.

As you might guess, by this time I had pretty well hit overload. When things slowed down, I sat down at the desk in the back room and began to think. The brain was racing and the imagination was working overtime. The P.L.O.M. (Poor Little Ol' Me) state of mind had taken over.

Then something came to mind. I remembered reading how Al Smith, a governor of New York, liked to answer his critics by saying: "Let's examine the record." I reached for pen and paper and listed all the things I thought had ganged up on me. You know what? In black and white they didn't seem quite so intimidating. Also, I couldn't help noticing how short the list was and all the things that were *not* on the list.

Could it be there really is something to Socrates' theory? He said that if the mass of humanity from the beginning of time were required to bring all their troubles and put them in a common pile, and then each person were required to take an equal portion from the pile, most would be happy to just take the problems they contributed and walk gratefully away.

BARBER-OSOPHY: Facts are generally much less intimidating than our imagination.

Coasting to Crisis Management

It was 6:30 A.M., and we had just finished having breakfast at McDonald's. Sherry had gone across the highway to Judson High School to set up for her first period math students. I was on FM 78, headed for the barbershop. All was well—until the car started losing power.

I immediately knew the problem, because I had just looked at the gas gauge and wondered if I would make it to work. Suddenly I got the answer.

Because of an aversion to walking in the dark and to the embarrassment of carrying a gas can to a stalled car, I forced myself to RELAX and to think—very quickly. If I could top the next hill, I could then coast downhill to a Diamond Shamrock.

So, I quickly shifted into neutral and hoped that no one pulled in front of me, forcing me to hit my brakes. Speaking of brakes, when the engine died, that was pretty much the end of the power brakes and the power steering. So, I braced myself to hit something cheap!

Fortunately, I was able to negotiate the turn into the driveway of the convenience store. But, I couldn't make it to the pump. Another problem!

I swallowed my pride and cautiously approached a stranger at the pump. "Sir, ah, I need to ask a favor." He looked like at me like he thought I was Jack the Ripper. "Could you please help me push my car up here. I've done a dumb thing and run out of gas." Instantly his features soften and he smiled as if to say, "Been there, done that." With his HELP, we pushed the car the short distance to the pump so that I could do what I should have done the night before.

After a very grateful "thank you" and a trip to the cashier, I was on my way. The 20-minute trip to the shop gave me time to think. First of all, I thought about the price of PROCRASTINATION. You see, the only reason for the crisis was because I had put off filling up. My grandpa used to say that it didn't cost a bit more to burn the top of the tank than it did the bottom. In this case money didn't have anything to do with it. The money I had for gas that morning was the same cash I had the night before.

Another thing that came to mind was the question of whether or not I would be able to open the shop on time after the unexpected delay. Though procrastination might be something I need to work on, TIME MAN-AGEMENT is not. I guess that's sort of a contradiction. What I mean is I'm rarely stressed by fear of being late. So, that's usually not a contributing factor in a crisis.

Though it's too late to make a long story short, let's just say everything worked out fine and the crisis turned out to be merely a tempest in a teapot.

BARBER-OSOPHY: Many a would-be crisis is defused by relaxing, by getting help or by a proper use of time to start with.

Doggin' It

"Never look a vicious dog in the eye. He will consider it a challenge."

Twice in two days I heard this advice from customers.

You can believe I was listening, because strange dogs and I don't get along too well. In fact, I've gotten hate mail from Snoopy.

When Sherry and I were first married, she immediately found out about this problem I have with other people's dogs. We had some friends whose dog would trap me in the car, while letting Sherry walk right to the front door of their home. If, as folks say, dogs can tell when you are afraid of them, this little dog must have enjoyed terrorizing me.

All of this reminds me of the fellow who had a similar problem and solved it with the only thing he had available—a pitchfork. While I certainly don't approve of such actions, the rest of the story is rather amusing.

When the man was taken to court by the owner of the dog, the judge asked him if he could possibly have come at the dog with the other end of the pitchfork.

"Yes, your honor," he replied, "provided he had come at me with the other end."

BARBER-OSOPHY: To avoid drastic measures, when possible, avoid desperate circumstances.

TOOLS

FOR A

HAPPY HOME

BARBER-OSOPHY: "A happy home is as close as we'll ever get to heaven on earth."

A Practical Guide to a
Better Marriage

A customer told me of a fellow whose wife told him she was leaving him for another man. The fellow's response was, "Is there anything I can do?" The wife replied, "Sure, you can give me a couple of weeks to find the right guy."

I laughed, as possibly you did, at an obvious joke. Then I began to ponder how Sherry and I have been able to stay married thirty-five years.

It is not because we were so mature when we married. I was not quite 20 and she was 18. Nor do I think we have stayed married because we are perfect individuals. I would be the first to tell you—Sherry is not perfect. Just kidding!

I do believe that there are some things that we have done right. We have utilized some concepts that have helped make our relationship work. These might be of help if utilized by others.

Before I tell you what these concepts are, let me say I'm not a marriage counselor. That might be to your advantage! At least it might keep me from being like the guy who had seven rules for raising kids, and then he had seven kids and had no rules. While there is certainly a place for counseling, there is the danger that advice can be long on theory and short on practical experience. With this in mind, I'll mention a few things that have worked for us.

1. The first concept involves commitment. From the start, we have been committed to making our marriage work. It has never been considered a trial relationship. Even when there are problems, it is assumed we can work them out and that bailing out is not an option.

2. Respect is equally important. Respect means refraining from anything that would cause one's spouse to lose face or to be embarrassed (especially in public). But it also means doing those little things that make the other person feel important and appreciated.

3. Communication has also been a huge part of our marriage. We have always been able to talk it out and it has kept us together, even at times when life has been a roller coaster. Unfortunately, many husbands and wives have walked when they should have talked.

4. Finally, though many other things could be mentioned, independence must be added to the list of things that work in marriage. Even though spouses come to naturally depend on each other for many

needs, healthy relationships provide for space— often. In children, smother love has been known to bring on asthma. In marriage it causes resentment.

As I said at the outset, these are concepts that have worked for us. You could probably add to the list. What we might add to the list would likely be additional manifestations of one common quality—absolute devotion to one's spouse.

BARBER-OSOPHY: The best advice in the world won't work if we won't.

"Everything I Need to Know About Raising Kids..."

While it's not entirely true that *"everything* I need to know about raising kids I learned behind a barber chair," it is true that I've learned *some things.*

I was reminded of these things after hearing a sad statement from a conscientious dad. He said that he and his son are now on different paths. I asked how old his son is. "Twelve," he answered. I thought of how close I am to Jon, our 22-year-old son, and how it would hurt me to think we were "on different paths" when he was twelve.

But, I also thought of the many kids who come through our doors and of the many parents who seem to be getting it right. Thus, I've developed sort of a "Barberosophy for Raising Good Kids." Here are a few such "Barber-osophies."

1. *Be in charge.* It doesn't seem possible that a 4-year-old child can control a 40-year-old parent. However, I've seen it happen, and it makes you wonder who is the child and who is the parent. It also makes you wonder if child abuse doesn't sometimes take the form of a parent who won't take charge.

2. *Reduce the choices*. While this is relative, depending on the age of the child, it seems that children who always have a choice regarding such things as treats and privileges tend to be ungrateful, unhappy and undisciplined. Sometimes it might be more appropriate if the choices are reduced to something I read on a friend's refrigerator: "This ain't Burger King. You take it my way or you don't get it at all."

3. *Be careful about showcasing the child*. There are far too many kids who receive no positive attention from anyone. There seems to be a growing number of parents, however, who make every interaction between their child and themselves a public event, a look-at-me-and/or-my-child situation. Thus, the child begins to think that the world revolves around him (her).

4. *Expect the best.* Parents who expect the first haircut to be "a piece of cake" are often rewarded. Similarly, by our words and actions we must always let our kids know we believe in them and expect the best from them. It propels them toward success.

BARBER-OSOPHY: Though there are no perfect parents or perfect children, it's easy to spot the parents who are genuinely trying to get it right.

A Generation of Hotdogs

"Congratulations! You're the proud parents of a bouncing, baby hotdog!"

Wouldn't it be something for a doctor to say that to a young couple? Yet, one never has for the simple reason showboats and hotdogs are not born. Their behavior is *learned*.

Such seemed to be the general opinion of customers in reaction to the "hot-dogging" that was displayed in a Little League World Series a few years ago. The actions of some of the Harlem players were clearly inappropriate, and the attempt by a commentator to downplay what had taken place was even more disgusting.

As the dad of a former Little Leaguer, I understand youthful immaturity and how "kids will be kids." But, on the other hand, what do we expect them to be? Old men? Horses or cows? Of course they will be kids. They will be kids who need guidance and proper examples in order to become respectable adults. With the influence of so many professional athletes and with little parental upbringing, I fear for their future.

Bum Phillips, former coach of the Houston Oilers, was once asked what he thought about players "dancing in the end zone." His words of wisdom were, as I recall, "I tell my players to give the football back to the official so that people don't think that's the first time you ever scored a touchdown." The star mentality, however, tends to exaggerate the importance of every achievement. When no one applauds daily accomplishments and egotism is a huge turn off, I wonder how these "stars" will cope.

There also comes a time when a person's value to society will generally be determined by contribution rather than self-promotion. This is somewhat like the Abraham Lincoln story of the fellow who put the fancy horn on his steamboat. Because of the amount of steam it took to blow the horn, every time the horn blew the boat stopped. In life, there are the doers and the horn blowers. Young folks, including athletes, especially need to learn this.

And then there is the proverb: "Pride goes before destruction, and a haughty spirit before a fall." (Proverbs 16:18) Our son once boasted of what he was going to do to another Little League all-star team when he pitched against them. He lasted about two innings. Because pride had lifted him so high, the fall took him a long way down.

Someone has said: "Be nice to everyone on your way up, because you will meet them again on your way down." Life has a way of humbling us and of sometimes causing us to see how greatly we depend on those for whom we once had so little regard.

BARBER-OSOPHY: Empty barrels make the most noise.

You've Gotta Love It

Never will I forget the day I came home from the barbershop and found Jon, who was fifteen at the time, hysterical with pain. He had just taken a baseball to the face.

While at practice, he was standing about twenty feet from home plate, soft-tossing to a teammate. The batter hit a line drive that struck Jon under his left eye, knocking him unconscious. The ball struck with such force that it wound up near the right field fence.

The next five to six hours were spent with doctors and technicians determining the extent of the damage. Fortunately there was no brain damage or serious eye damage; but it was determined Jon would need plastic surgery to repair what is called orbital blowout.

Since the surgeon said it would be a week before the swelling and blood would go down enough to permit surgery, Jon immediately wanted to know if he could play ball. In fact, all along he had asked that question as he sobbed in pain. So, he played in three games between the injury and the surgery, pitching a complete game the night before the operation. But when he came out of surgery, the physician said that was the end of his season.

Though the injury hurt, I think it hurt more to be told his season was over—since Jon ate, slept and breathed baseball. From the time Jon was a small boy, he said he is going to be a pro pitcher. He worked extremely hard to achieve his goal. He even battled back after going though rehab to rebuild a rotator cuff injury that occurred when he was eleven.

Did he reach his goal? Not that one. His career goal changed. And that's okay. But, whatever he is able to attain in the future will be as a result of the same passion for what he's doing and the same intensity of desire that he had for baseball.

BARBER-OSOPHY: Wherever it is possible for us to go, passion will take us there.

A Few Thoughts From the Hill

It's fun to listen to parents and students talk about college plans. We have some very bright, talented young folks who come into the barbershop.

I'm always reminded of the time two dads were discussing their college students. One commented that all students are independent until the 30th of the month. Ain't it the truth!

We enjoyed a big day at our house when our third and last student signed his letter of intent to play college baseball. Though he was certainly not the first or last student or athlete to earn a scholarship, we felt like he was. It was an emotional time.

On the same day, while I was working in the back yard, my attention was drawn to one corner of the yard—to our pitcher's mound. Memories shot through my mind like a Nolan Ryan fastball.

I was reminded of the time I was catching Jon, and he broke my toe with a curveball. Then there was also the shot to my eye, causing me to have to cut hair nearly one-eyed the next day.

Most vivid are the shared emotions, the ups and downs—the tears and the joy, that go with a shared dream.

Even during those occasions when our teenager and we, his parents, had a strong difference of opinion, there was always a strong bond and a common interest. Often all it took to set feelings right was, "You want to pitch?"

Not too long ago, I heard of a study that determined American parents spend an average of seven minutes *a week* one on one with their children. I'm thankful I'm not part of that statistic, and I hope you're not either.

BARBER-OSOPHY: No one ever looks back on his or her life and says, "I sure wish I had spent less time with my children."

OUT OF THE MOUTHS OF BABES

When I tell something about one of our children, I'm reminded of the two strangers who were seated next to each other on a flight. Just before they landed, they commented to one another about what a nice visit they had. Then one of them added, "However, I didn't get around to showing you pictures of my grandchildren, did I?" "No, and I really appreciate it," came the reply.

Yet, sometimes we can't resist telling stories about our children. Presently, the urge comes to me one more time as a result of a conversation I had with a young man about what grade he was in. As he told me he was going into the third grade, I was reminded of when our son was in the first grade.

Jon, who is now twenty-two, was in the first grade twice. Because his birthday is August 29th, he barely made the age deadline for starting school and was not mature enough at the time. So, he was held back instead of being promoted to the second grade. As you might guess, it was a sad time when we had to tell him he had not been promoted.

As an illustration of how resilient children can be, while Jon was in the first grade for the second time, his grandmother overheard the following conversation between Jon and a visitor at church:

"What's your name?" the visitor asked.

"Jon."

"How old are you, Jon?" was the visitors next question.

"Seven."

The gentleman asked, "What grade are you in?"

Again, with simple directness, Jon said, "First."

With friendly encouragement, the visitor quipped, "I'll bet that's really a tough grade, isn't it?

"No, sir, not really," Jon replied. "This is my second time there."

With the disappointment and embarrassment of perceived failure ended, the let-it-all-hang-out frankness of a child prevailed. An adult might have been too humiliated to share details and just said, "No, it's not tough," and then changed the subject. But, not a child.

In this regard, we need to remember our childhood. We all suffer setbacks. At times, we fail. This is a long way from being a failure. A failure is a person who simply refuses to "get over it" and just "gives up."

BARBER-OSOPHY: Avoid being a failure—get over it!

If Grandpa Did It

Someone has said that the shortest measurable portion of time is the time between when the light in front of you turns to green and the guy behind you blows his horn. Maybe we could call that a light-second.

This came to mind one day as I made my way from the barbershop to a mail center a few blocks away. The light changed, and before I had time to blink—"Toot!"

I could have done what an old gentleman I once knew did. When his car stalled, the lady in the car behind his just leaned on her horn. He simply got out of his car, stepped to her window, and said, "Lady, tell you what. I'll sit here and blow your horn if you'll go up there and start my car."

Sometimes when people are so impatient, we think we might like to do such a thing. In this case, however, my irritation was cooled just a bit by a pleasant memory of my maternal grandfather.

One of the things our family always got a kick out of, and that we still joke about, is how Grandpa Sanders loved his car horn. It was nearly impossible for the person in front of him to get away from the light before Grandpa would tap his horn, "Toot, toot." And it was always just like that—two light taps. That is, unless the situation got critical. Then he would stick his head out the window and holler at the driver. Yet, this impatient, dear man would have given a needy person the shirt off his back.

So, when I was inclined to have a bad attitude toward a stranger who did something my grandfather did quite often, I asked myself how I would have reacted if it had been Grandpa.

BARBER-OSOPHY: Treat everyone like family, and you're less likely to mistreat anyone.

If It's Good—Savor It

Over the years, hordes of people have asked how I gathered the material or came up with the concept for "Barber-osophy." Well, maybe not hordes. Mom asked me once.

Anyway, I'm always glad to be asked because it gives me an opportunity to relate something positive.

The book and the concept are the product of a tradition Sherry and I started years ago. Around New Year's Eve we check into a hotel, as a means of getting away from the holiday stress and as a way of celebrating the accomplishments of the year.

To help us recall the year's events, we usually find a quiet spot in the hotel restaurant where we can enjoy a cup of coffee while reading my journal for the preceding year. As we read, pleasant memories of things forgotten come alive.

This journal idea was started years ago as a means of heightening my personal awareness of life. I've found that too often we are able to recall so little of even pleasant events after weeks or months have dulled the memory. This is a way of keeping the memories alive. Since I record very few of the unpleasant events, we are able to accentuate the positive, while adding zest to our 35-year marriage.

It is also a great way to write "Barber-osophy" because in connection with my personal journal I also began recording the wonderful things that take place in the barbershop. Soon a journal became a book and in time Mom's question could become hordes of inquirers.

BARBER-OSOPHY: Be on the lookout for ways to keep the good stuff alive. It could be the difference between really living, and a life of quiet desperation.

A Little Seasoning

The week before Christmas is usually one of the busiest times of the year at J.B.'s Barber Shop. It seems that everyone wants to look nice for family, photos and parties. So, we look forward to the increase in business. However, I must admit that I don't generally look forward to the holiday, as such.

For years, Sherry and the kids considered me kind of a Scrooge. Thus, they learned to just tolerate my annual moodiness.

I finally reached a point where I felt guilty about my immaturity and how it affected the rest of the family. I decided to try to identify the source of the problem.

I soon discovered that part of the problem had to do with the "traditional compulsories"—the excessive buying, eating, visiting, etc. The other part involved how holidays disrupt my routine.

When in town, my routine is very simple: get out of bed at 5:25 A.M., leave the house by 5:50, be in a restaurant drinking coffee and reading a book by 6 and open the shop at 7 A.M. Yet, holidays change all this and leave me with an uncomfortable "What do I do now?" type of uselessness.

With our three children married and gone from home and with other loved ones having passed on, there has been a change in attitude. Scrooge has slowly turned into a sentimentalist, as holidays take on a meaning they never had. They've become those precious moments on a clock that can never be turned back.

Horace Mann once ran a lost-and-found advertisement: "Lost, one 24-carat golden day. Each hour studded with 60 diamond minutes. Each minute studded with 60 ruby seconds. But don't bother to look for it. It is gone forever, that wonderful, golden day, I lost today."

BARBER-OSOPHY: Mature people appreciate the timeless benefits that "a little seasoning" brings to a routine.

CUTTING

UP

"Against the assault of humor
nothing can stand." – Mark Twain

THE ASSAULT OF HUMOR

Occasionally, customers ask how long J.B.'s Barber Shop has been open. The shop opened on July 25th, 1956. This year we hope to complete 48 years, as we move toward our Golden Anniversary.

Some of our customers may still remember our 40th anniversary. For us, it brings back fond memories of flowers, balloons, family, friends, coffee, punch and a huge chocolate cake decorated as a barber pole. The local media gave us nice coverage and many friends came by or called. It was great!

For me it was also the beginning of a very busy week. That was the very same week that Sherry and I celebrated our 27th wedding anniversary. We decided since I had a speaking engagement that weekend in Austin, we would combine the engagement with a get-away weekend.

After Sherry had settled into the hotel room, I headed for the convention. After the speech, I recall feeling a little like the rabbit that had a skunk for a playmate. After a week, he said he had enjoyed about all he could stand. Though it was a great week, the normal routine, plus the extras, had taken their toll and I was just glad the week was over and that I was able to relax in the hotel room with Sherry.

As I began to reflect on the week's events, something came to mind that placed everything in perspective. It involved a crusty old veteran who was part of the Veterans of Foreign War convention that I had just addressed. He was sitting right in front of the speaker's platform.

After the presentation, he paid me a rather nice compliment. Because of his very colorful language, I'll not quote him word for word. As he was vigorously pumping my hand, he said that when he read in the program that they were going to have a motivational speaker, he turned to those at his table and asked, "What is a motivational speaker? Is that someone who just sort of blows smoke?" Then, with a twinkle in his eye, he said, "Tonight I sure learned what a motivational speaker is."

Believe me, I know what it is to bomb as a speaker. I've been there and will probably be there again. On this occasion, however, everything seemed to click.

The next morning as I was sitting in the hotel restaurant drinking coffee and reading, I came across something that seemed to explain why things had clicked. I read that Mark Twain said, "Against the assault of humor nothing can stand." I guess that would apply even to my friend who didn't like motivational speakers.

If, as someone has said, the strongest nation in the world is imagination, the strongest force affecting attitudes must be humor. It has tremendous power to break down walls of prejudice and to ease everyday pressures. Give it a try next time opposition or stress seems overwhelming.

BARBER-OSOPHY: Never underestimate the power of humor.

Humor Can Be a Funny Thing

"Dad, you'd heard that before, hadn't you?" I had to confess I had. "Then why didn't you stop me?" she asked.

"Because if I stopped everyone who started telling me a joke I had already heard, I wouldn't have any friends."

This was the conversation that took place between Amanda, our youngest daughter, and me several years ago. I went on to tell her that though I have definite weaknesses, one of my strengths is that I enjoy good stories so much that I never forget one. Unless it is a story that is "fresh out of the box" (and it rarely is), I've heard it and remember it. But, I listen and laugh anyway partly out of courtesy, and partly I simply love to laugh.

Customers will tell you that I have, at times, been known to pull their leg for the sake of laughter. That can have a funny way of backfiring, however.

Recently, a doctor who frequents J.B.'s was seated in one of our waiting chairs. In walked an attractive young lady who resembled him and seated herself next to him. Naturally, I figured she was his daughter, but I didn't ask for fear he might tell me she was his wife. That sort of thing can happen with children and grandchildren, as well.

When it came the doctor's turn for his haircut, he quietly got in the chair. Toward the end of his haircut, I looked up and noticed that the young lady was looking toward us and smiling as if she approved of his haircut. I smiled and asked if she would like to finish the haircut. She kind of laughed. He did not.

As if that weren't bad enough, when I had finished I looked at her and said that the doctor looked so nice he ought to take her to lunch—in a very fine restaurant. Again, she laughed a little. He did not.

After he got out of the chair and paid me, I realized why my humor had not been quite appreciated. He walked right out without saying a word to her—because he didn't know her from Adam! He probably thought we now had some new sort of matchmaker service. The young lady, on the other hand, had just come in to get her hair trimmed.

BARBER-OSOPHY: Careless humor has its price.

Caution—Amateur at Work!

Mom and I recently decided to combine errands and to run them together on Monday, the day the shop is closed. One of her errands involved taking her sewing machine to the repair shop. First, I needed to take it out of the cabinet for her.

Even though it's well known in our family that my mechanical skills are a tad "underdeveloped," I figured I could handle such a small assignment. I crawled under the machine and, with the confidence that goes with ignorance, proceeded to loosen the screws that held the sewing machine in the cabinet. It wasn't as easy as I thought!

Next thing I knew, while the machine was raised so that I could inspect the situation and decide on a procedure, "Bang!" It slammed down on my finger. "Yeow!!!"

As I'm flat of my back and writhing in pain, I hear Mom ask, "Are you okay?" Not wanting to make her feel badly, I mumbled, "I'll be alright." Then I crawled from under the machine and gently inspected the injury.

My finger was already throbbing and blood oozed from under the nail. A blood blister appeared in a dark crimson streak under the skin extending about a half inch out from the nail. The finger was already swelling.

Oh, it hurt! Just running water over it as I stood at the bathroom sink made it feel so much better.

I pulled myself back together and removed the sewing machine. Together we ran errands on an otherwise pleasant morning.

After the errands were done and I was driving home from Mom's, I began to think about the mishap.

For some strange and comical reason what first came to mind was, "If one member suffers, all suffer together..." (1 Corinthians 12:26). Boy, could I testify to that! When the left hand grabbed the injured finger, the face grimaced in pain, the blood started to ooze and the feet carried me to the bathroom sink...all the members were getting into the act.

This, in turn, brought to mind the relative importance of events. At the time, it seemed like a big deal. But, as I drove home, it wasn't such a crisis. It was only a badly smashed finger. It hurt like the "dickens" for a little while, but it soon quit hurting. So it is with certain things in life. The misfortunes soon quit hurting, but if we keep replaying them in our minds and in our conversations, they become much bigger than they really are.

Another thing I thought of was the importance of little things. The first thought I had after my head cleared from the initial pain was, "Will I be able to cut hair?" The injury only involved my index finger on my right hand, but if my finger were broken or if it remained swollen and painful, that could be a problem. It could affect my ability to work, which would in turn affect my income. That's a problem! But, none of that was the case simply because I was lucky. Had I been paying attention to little things to start with, luck wouldn't have been necessary. We hear so much about not neglecting little things, lest they become big things, but it's still good advice.

Lastly, the incident reminded me that when something is out of my field, I must always proceed with caution. Otherwise, it could result in more than a hurt finger.

BARBER-OSOPHY: A bad haircut is not the only sign of an amateur's work.

Enough is Enough

Years ago, I read the story of a couple who, having been married for 50 years, decided to get a divorce. The judge was flabbergasted by their decision. He asked the old gentleman, "How can you folks come to this decision after so many years of marriage? What would cause you to do this?"

"Very simple," the old fellow replied. "Enough is enough!"

At J.B.'s we have our version of this story.

An old-timer and longtime customer (now deceased) walked in and was greeted by J.B.

"How ya doin today, Al?"

The man's reply came as a total surprise to J.B. He very quietly asked, "Why do you call me Al?"

"I thought that was your name," J.B. said.

"My name's not Al," he replied. "My name is John."

After the fellow received his haircut and walked to his car, J.B. turned to me and began laughing.

"That's unbelievable! He let me call him Al for thirty years."

I guess he'd had enough.

BARBER-OSOPHY: If it ain't right, the simple passing of time won't change a thing.

JUMP START A SMILE

Because Saturdays can be incredibly busy at J.B.'s Barber Shop, anything that brings a smile is often a great stress reliever. For that reason, a story I had heard earlier in the week came in handy.

The story involves a guy who tried to get into a fancy restaurant but was told he couldn't enter without a tie. So, after unsuccessfully pleading his case, he finally went to his car, pulled his jumper cables out of the truck and tied them around his neck. He returned to the restaurant and told the fellow at the door that he now had a tie.

The attendant still had some misgivings about the situation, but finally agreed to let the fellow in. However, he did make one more demand, "Just don't start anything!"

The customer I told this to seemed to enjoy it. He paid for his haircut in spite of the story. After telling him the story, though, I added, "There's this friend that I can't wait to tell that to. He always has a story for me."

The friend I was referring to never seems to get down or depressed. Even when he lost his wife, though he went through the usual grieving period, it wasn't long before he was the same upbeat, positive fellow who always has a laugh line.

In this respect he is much like the man who initially told me the necktie story. His wife was undergoing chemotherapy at the time, and together they were going through a very tough period.

Yet, in both cases these friends managed to keep their own spirits up simply by lifting the spirits of others. While we are not surprised to find that it happens that way, what we often fail to see is that this action involves courage.

BARBER-OSOPHY: It's an uncommon courage that makes another smile while carrying a heavy burden.

When We are Blind-sided by Miscommunication

During the summer at J.B.'s we see lots of changes and moves. With June weddings, transfers and end of school, this is to be expected.

I'm reminded of the time, not too long ago, when my parents moved. For them it was a very difficult time. They were leaving the home they had occupied for forty-three years and where they had reared my brother and me.

From the beginning, I was excited for them. Not only were they having a new home built and moving into a much better neighborhood, but they would also be only ten minutes away from us.

When I had a few minutes between customers, I would call to see how things were going. Sometimes they would stop by the barbershop and give me up-dates, as I was cutting Dad's hair.

If you have ever had a house built, you understand how frustrating and stressful it can be. So, they shared lots of stories of agony and ecstasy.

The house was finally completed and ready for them to move in. With that came detail after detail, one of which was window treatments.

About this time my parents were showing signs of wear. Fortunately, they were able to find a salesman who was unusually helpful with the window blinds. He was so nice Mom began to think maybe she had solved another problem. Maybe this gentleman could hang the blinds for them.

She turned to the fellow and casually asked, "You don't hang blinds on the side, do you?" The man's answer turned out to be just the stress reliever they needed. With no hint of having misunderstood her question, he responded, "Oh, no ma'am. I don't hang blinds on the side. I always hang them from the top."

BARBER-OSOPHY: Miscommunication, like most things in life, can often have a humorous side.

Useless (but fun) Information from our Unscientific Poll

One of my favorite statements is: "It ain't what a man don't know that makes him a fool, but what he does know that ain't so."—Josh Billings. This quote reminds me to be correct in what I say and also to be sure the information I receive is accurate.

Concerning accuracy, it makes no difference whether information is received via radio, TV, newspaper, the Internet or some trusted person. Source doesn't assure accuracy.

What about information that's reliable, but of no practical value? Surely, it's okay to learn something just for the sake of knowing or just for the fun of it.

At this point you might say, "Okay, but what's your point?" So glad you asked. I've been setting you up for some semi-accurate, though useless, information, from our unofficial poll at J.B.'s Barber Shop.

Q. What's the number one topic at J.B.'s?
 A. The weather.

Q. Do customers prefer cold weather or hot weather?
 A. Yes.

Q. What's the most common complaint about a haircut?
 A. Too short.

Q. What's the most common question people ask about hair?

    A. What do you do with the hair you sweep up?

Q. What's the age of J.B.'s oldest customer?

    A. He was almost 104.

Q. What sport do customers like most?

    A. Hunting.

Q. What, besides hair, is most often left in the barbershop?

    A. Caps.

Q. What's the most popular section of the newspaper?

    A. Sports.

Q. What's the least popular section of the newspaper?

    A. Classified.

Q. What's the greatest source of joy to customers?

    A. Their kids.

Q. What's the greatest source of misery to customers?

    A. Their kids.

Q. What items in J.B.'s Barber Shop have drawn the most comment?

    A. The enormous steer horns and the photograph of Nolan Ryan taking on Robin Ventura, when Ventura decided to charge the mound.

BARBER-OSOPHY: Though all information should be accurate, not all must be usable.

FOR MORE INFORMATION
ABOUT SPEAKING ENGAGEMENTS
BY TERRY SUMERLIN

☎ CALL 210-661-2053

To Order Copies

BARBER-OSOPHY—
HAIR WE GO AGAIN
AND/OR
BARBER-OSOPHY—
SHEAR SUCCESS FOR YOUR CUTTING EDGE

☎ **Telephone Orders:** Call 1-800-329-3381
Fax Orders: 210-828-5330
✉ **Postal Orders:** S E Publishing
   6338 N. New Braunfels, PMB 180
   San Antonio, Texas 78209

Please send check with order.
$12.95 for each book
Texas Residents Add $1.05 tax
$2.00 postage for one book—
add 50 cents for each additional book.

Send _____ copies of *Barber-osophy—Hair We Go Again*
Send _____ copies of *Barber-osophy—Shear Success*

_____

_____

_____

Thank you for your order.
For speaking engagements, call
Terry Sumerlin at 210-661-2053

www.ingramcontent.com/pod-product-compliance
Lightning Source LLC
Chambersburg PA
CBHW052138170626
46812CB00004B/1496